CUPCAKE QUEENS

A COMFORT FOOD ROMANCE

DARLENE EVERLY

❀ Created with Vellum

Hardcover: ISBN 978-1-954719-14-9

Paperback: ISBN 978-1-954719-13-2

Ebook: ISBN 978-1-954719-12-5

First paperback edition August 2021.

Edited by Jupiter Alley.

Cover art by Jupiter Alley.

Layout by Wishing Well Books.

WA, US

✻ Created with Vellum

DARLENE EVERLY

Cupcake Queens

A COMFORT FOOD ROMANCE

For the Queens

Personal Pan was just the beginning of the Comfort Food romances, now here's Cupcake Queens! If you would like to be the first to hear about the next book in the series titled Brewed Anew, get a free book and an exclusive short story in this series, as well as see what else the author has written, please go to darleneeverly.com and sign up for her newsletter.

Happily Ever Baking!

"Alright," I said, hitching up my toolbox, leaning it against my hip, and grabbing the bag full of garbage parts I was going to take back to the shop with me to dispose of. "I'm all done here, Ruth. I'll have the bill sent over to you, okay?"

The tiny elderly lady pushed herself up from the chair next to the ornate, antique fireplace. Her living room was wallpapered in a pattern that must have been as old as the building—which meant it was probably older than Ruth. It was soft and dusty rose like everything else.

A weird little part of me wondered what came first, the color scheme of the rest of the place, or the wallpaper.

It was so damn hot in there that I had a hard time stopping myself from wiping the sweat from my brow. My hands were probably dusted with fiberglass shards from the bit of batting insulation I had to deal with, and the last thing I wanted was an itchy forehead for an entire night. How Ruth withstood the proximity to the blaze crackling away in the fireplace I would never know.

"Oh, Theresa," Ruth said, smiling at me and coming to my

side. She reached up and patted a hand on my shoulder. It barely registered it was so insubstantial. "Thank you so much for fixing it for me. Tell your mother to come see me soon, okay?"

"Yes, of course I will." I smiled back at her and made my way out to the narrow hallway in her building.

Good thing there were only two other tenants in the two-story home converted to apartments, otherwise it might have been impossible to navigate around someone I ran into on my way out the door. I had no idea why Ruth lived in a two story and didn't find a place without stairs, or at least an elevator.

My knee yelled at me as I walked down the steps. I gritted my teeth, my grip on the toolbox and the garbage bag tightening. It would have been better if I could have held onto the railing like I did on the way up, but there was too much in my hands.

All I could do was make my way down and grumble about it inside my head.

Hopefully, next week I would only have first floor places to go to. Icing it usually helped, but I still didn't want to overwork it and injure it further. The damn brace on it sure seemed more useless than helpful.

My mother would have been admiring the woodwork on the staircase and the stained-glass transom over the front door, but all I admired was the flat ground when I got down to the first floor.

Once at the truck outside, I put my overly heavy toolbox on the floor of the jump seat area and grabbed a wet wipe to scrub my hands on. In a perfect world, it would snag all the pokey shards of fiberglass off my hands. But it never worked that way because the world was a lot of things, and none of them were perfect.

My phone chimed in my pocket, and I pulled it out before using my good leg to jump into the front seat.

Sitting in the truck again, I sighed. Taking the weight off my knee allowed muscles nowhere near my leg to relax too.

My phone chimed again.

Olivia and Campbell have the night off. See you at Best.

I leaned my head against the seat.

Why did my friends feel the need to get together tonight? Why couldn't they just let me go home, ice my knee, and sit in a hot bath until tomorrow?

Doesn't everyone have to work in the morning?

Texting that back to Katie was a risk, she wasn't likely to take no for an answer regardless of what excuse I tried. It exhausted me just thinking about it.

Hello ding dong. Tomorrow is Saturday. Do you have to work on a Saturday? Do I need to call your mother?

Crap. Well, there went that excuse.

I have to shower first.

Because no one wanted me around without getting all the bits and pieces of work off of me, and I didn't want to be around anyone until I did that either.

Putting the bag with the garbage in it on the floor in the passenger seat wheel well, I set down my phone, and checked for a break in the traffic to pull the not-practical-at-all-for-the-city truck out onto the road.

A little red car had a huge space behind it, and I was about to pull into it when my phone chimed again.

I glanced down at my phone for only a second, but by the time I looked up again the space was full of other cars.

Of course it was.

Maybe I should have just leaned back and taken a nap. Maybe I wasn't meant to get out of this parking spot. I really shouldn't have been able to get this parking spot in the first place. Maybe this was my penance for that good fortune.

It made sense. Nothing good came without something negative riding within it.

Like a scholarship to your first-choice school for cheerleading, and then blowing out your knee at your first game.

The phone chimed again, and I swear it sounded like Katie scolding me.

It's your turn to pick up dessert.

Deacon says The Bake Place.

Gluten free, too.

Deacon says give him all the gluten.

I smiled. Deacon and I thought alike.

Maybe it was petty to laugh and type out a snarky text. But I deleted it, so I gave myself a pass on my moment as Mayor of Petty Land. Instead, I just texted back, "k."

The Bake Place though…I couldn't quite remember where it was. Pike Place?

While I could have texted Katie back, or Olivia, or any of my friends, if I had to drive around a little bit before I found it, the less direct route might give me more time to rest my knee before I had to walk on it again.

Once I found it, I remembered why I didn't come here.

It wasn't *near* Pike Place. It was *in* Pike Place Market.

Crap.

Driving the truck meant I had to park way too far away. The streets of Seattle ran up and down steep hills, and right around Pike Place was no different than other areas in that regard.

The last thing I needed was to the hike through the neighborhood on my bad knee.

"Nope. Not taking orders today," I said to the empty truck.

I turned the truck back toward home, a cleanup, an order to

have desert delivered to me, and an awaiting call to someone to pick me up.

Done for the day, to me, meant not driving the behemoth anymore either.

But part of me was sad I wouldn't get to try the famous desserts from The Bake Place. One day, one day I would have the time and the right car.

A pothole sent a jarring bump through the truck that made my knee scream and forced me to suck in a hissing breath through my teeth.

Maybe I would have to wait for the imaginary day when my knee felt better to go to the bakery.

CEECEE

I was never going to be able to get out of the bakery.

Marcus wasn't there to cover me, and I had to pee.

Doing the potty dance discreetly while trying to help people with their baked goods was not how I thought the day was going to go.

But I couldn't afford to turn the sign in the window and lose the last sales of the day. Not on a normal day, and definitely not when the fridge was broken.

"Ceecee I was so sorry to hear about your mom," Mrs. Williams said, her dark brown eyes growing misty.

I smiled, although it was brittle, and I knew it. There was no way to force my face to allow room for a full, robust smile when someone brought up my mom. It didn't matter that it happened four months ago. I wasn't sure I would ever be able to be shiny and truly happy when her death was mentioned. And especially not right now.

"Thank you, Mrs. Williams," I said, wrapping up her usual order.

She reached across the counter to pat my hand with her heavily lined one.

Mrs. Williams didn't show her advanced age in her face. Her dark skin was still flawless, and she kept a head wrap on at all times so no gray hair showed to place her age either. But her years of life and experience were written all over her hands.

"You know, I came as soon as we got back to Seattle. This is my first stop after my house." Her smile was so kind it was easy to let go of the flare of frustration inside telling me to yell at her to please stop talking about it.

"Allison was a wonderful woman, and I'm so glad you've taken over the bakery. This city wouldn't be the same without The Bake Place and your famous cinnamon rolls." She handed me a wad of cash and picked up her boxes of treats.

"Mrs. Williams, I appreciate you saying that. This bakery means a lot to me." With my lip between my teeth, I shifted my weight from one foot to the other, fighting off the pressure of the tears that waited at the backs of my eyes while attempting not to pee my pants.

I tried to hand her the change, but she folded my fingers around the money and winked at me.

"If I was here instead of in Arizona, I would have given this to you then to help with the funeral expenses." She smiled and turned to go.

"No, Mrs. Williams," I said, rushing to the half door that led from behind the counter to the front of the shop.

"Listen, Ceecee, when George passed, your mom helped me." She smiled and looked down at the wedding ring she still wore five years after his death, before lifting her face to mine. Her smile changed to one that said tears were waiting in her eyes too. "Your mother was a good one, and I am honored I got to call her friend."

She nodded and I nodded back, my vision swimming in the tears I kept back by sheer force of will.

The chime over the door sounded and I moved back behind the glass cases filled with the last of the day's treats and a couple loaves of bread. Once there, I leaned against the wall next to the short swinging door.

"Hey, Ceecee," Olivia said, the chime sounding as Mrs. Williams made her way out. Olivia's voice was bright, and the smell of her family's pizza restaurant wafted in with her.

"Olivia," I said, truly happy to see her as I got the waiting tears under control and a smile back on my face that I hoped wasn't melancholy anymore. I shoved the cash into the pocket of my apron. "No Campbell today?"

"Campbell is in the car. He's doing the circle instead of finding parking," she said, her face shining the minute his name was mentioned. Campbell and Olivia were relationship goals.

"So, what's on for tonight then? I only have one cinnamon roll left." I shouldn't have had any left. On normal days they were gone by ten in the morning, but business had been slow since the road work caused everyone to avoid the market.

"Well, I'm for sure taking that." She grinned at me and then bent to peer in the glass cases, her brown eyes sparkling. "I also think I'm going to clean you out of everything else in here."

"No, you're not," I said with a chuckle and a good-natured roll of my eyes. She had a plethora of free food she could have had from her own restaurant, or Campbell's aunt if she wanted something different.

"Yes," she said, nodding with her eyebrows high, "I am. I'm heading to karaoke with Deacon and some others. He'll eat all of this if we let him. Hey, you should come."

She looked serious, but I just shook my head.

"Thanks, Olivia, but I'm beat. And Marcus doesn't come in tomorrow until the afternoon." All of that was true, but I didn't want to tell her that I didn't have any money to chip in for something like that. And I really didn't want to take up all the space in the room. An intrusion from me was a little more substantial than an intrusion from someone Olivia's size.

While trying to ignore the assessing look on her face, I started packaging up her purchases.

"Can you turn the sign on the window?" I asked, looking past her and pointing.

"No problem. And I understand tired, but Ceecee, you really should get out a little more. You know half my friends haven't even met you and they would love you." She took out her phone and tapped away at it before looking back at me with a discerning gaze I really didn't like at that moment.

"Did my mom ask you to tell me that before she left?" I asked, trying for lighthearted but ending up somewhere just this side of sad.

She cocked her head to the side and narrowed her eyes at me, her lips pursing just a bit. Which, if I was being honest, made her really hot and left me blinking before I could focus again on what I was doing.

Campbell was a lucky guy.

If I had known she was pansexual before we saw each other at Pride, then I would have asked her out. She started dating Campbell before that, though. But we didn't know each other as well back then and the story of her dating history never came up until we were marching side-by-side in our ostentatious best. By then she already had the only boyfriend I thought was good enough for her.

"You know, if you came with us, you would be doing me a favor," she said, her face glued to her phone as if she wasn't stooping to dirty tricks by appealing to my sense of curiosity.

"Haha. Okay, why would I be doing you a favor?" I shook my head and smiled.

"Because," she looked up at me, her face alight like a cat about to snatch a mouse, "My ex, Theresa, will be there and she is not only tone deaf, but she's had a rough couple months. So, if you come along, she would have to get out of her funk and be her old self for a new person, and I would get the added bonus of not having to listen to her sing."

I laughed.

Bent over to lean on the counter, I laughed until I almost peed my pants and had to stop abruptly.

"Olivia, I have to go to the bathroom, can you wait just a sec?" I was moving to the restroom in the hall before she even waved her hand at me to go.

The relief was divine. It was silly of me to wait so long, but it turned out worth it to sell everything from the cases.

Getting up and pulling up my pants, I leaned over to flush and nothing happened.

"What the hell?" I muttered, taking off the lid on the back of the tank. There was no water in the tank in the back.

"How the hell did that happen?" I bent down to look at the pipe connecting the toilet to the wall. There was a crack in it.

Looking behind me at the grate in the middle of the painted concrete floor of the bathroom, I reached my hand to the spot under the pipe, it was wet.

Fantastic. No water at all.

Not only was I not going to get to go with Olivia and have at least one night of a life, but I was going to have to learn how to do plumbing. I couldn't be without water for very long. Perfect.

"Ceecee? Can I use the bathroom when you're done?" Olivia called from the other side of the door.

Washing my hands in the sink, I tried to think of a way to tell her without telling her how bad it was. How I couldn't get a plumber. But there was no way not to at least partially lie.

"I'm sorry, Olivia," I said, walking out of the bathroom and shaking my head. "A pipe is busted and I'm going to have to turn off my main water."

"Oh, Ceecee." Her eyes got huge, and she looked like I just told her a tornado was outside. In Seattle. Actually it was only almost as devastating. "Let me call a friend of mine."

"Why?" Of all the things I thought she would say, that wasn't one of them.

"She works for a contractor. If she doesn't know how to fix it, she will know someone who does." She was already back to tapping on her phone.

"No," I said, my voice too loud and too rough.

The look on her face was so concerned it almost looked like fear. Crap.

"Sorry, I just mean that you don't have to ruin your night for me. I can call my guy in the morning. I have to call an appliance repair guy for the fridge too. And I'll call the building's owner. It's not a big deal."

Olivia cocked her head at me and narrowed her eyes.

"I already texted my friend, but if you are that tired then I'll have her come by in the morning. She'll just fix the water, have a look at the fridge, and you can trust her. We're friends. It's what we do for each other."

"Thanks," I said, wondering how much it was going to cost me to have such a good friend.

Maybe my mother's wedding ring.

All I could hope was that it would be enough to pay off the repairs to the water and the fridge. Because after that, there wasn't anything left.

"So, tell me again why I just had to lie to my mother, drive myself here, and go to work rescuing some bakery tomorrow before any sane person should be awake in the morning?" I asked, leaning into Deacon's side as he handed me another ridiculously yummy sugar glazed something.

"Because the bakery in question is my favorite and made all the treats you're shoving in your face," Katie said, sticking her tongue out at me before popping a bite of some garlicky roll thing in her mouth.

"And," Olivia said, looking at both of us like we were naughty children. "You are a good person and want to be nice to my friend."

"Now you're playing dirty," Campbell said, leaning over to kiss Olivia.

I shook my head and smiled. Those two were so cute it made me want to puke sometimes, but they were also two of the best people I knew and deserved to be happy.

Especially after how I messed it up with Olivia when I was the one she was kissing.

Campbell was an upgrade from me. Of that I was certain.

"Fine, I'll go, but I hope this friend of yours has more of these there," I said, winking at Olivia who clapped her hands together.

"Never play poker, Olivia," Deacon said with a laugh that rumbled through his massive chest and shook me in my spot.

"Oh, is that what you do when the season is over?" Katie asked, her eyes bright and a big grin on her face that made me sit up and put distance between me and her cousin.

Deacon was a giant football player for the University of Washington, but I knew them both well enough to know that she was the one to fear. And weird, overly happy Katie, was definitely in the 'this can only end badly' category.

"Um," Deacon mumbled, going rigid, his hand holding a bite of some kind of bread inches from his face, suspended in the air. If it was possible for a black man to turn white, he did, his eyes darting around the room like he was looking for a way out.

"I'm sure my dads would love to hear that." She paused, her smile only growing wider, and Deacon already looked like he was going to be sick. "And so would your mom."

"No. No, I've only played it a couple times with the guys. Please don't tell anyone. Katie, come on." Deacon was stammering, leaning closer and closer to his cousin, his hands actually shaking.

"Katie, come on. Leave him alone. You're just messing with him," I said, shaking my head and reaching for the binder of songs on the coffee table.

"Theresa, geez, fine," Katie said, raising her hands and backing away as if she was afraid of me.

I looked around the room, even behind myself, trying to figure out what the hell she was doing.

"You don't have to punish me by singing something," she

said, and Olivia's mouth popped open while Campbell cringed and Deacon recoiled.

"What crawled up your butt, Katie? I know I'm tone deaf, but no one cares. It's just us. First, you go after Deacon, and now me? Seriously, what is wrong with you right now?" Maybe I should have been a little less harsh because she wilted in front of me, her eyes growing watery with unshed tears. But someone had to call her out on this thing she was doing lately because it was miserable to be around her.

Her mouth fell open and then worked around words that didn't come out.

The seconds grew longer, and I wasn't sure anymore if I was the one who had crossed the line. By the looks on everyone's faces, no one was sure what to do.

"I…" Katie said, finally breaking the silence, her voice small and quavering, "I'm sorry. I…Um, I think I need to go home and get some sleep."

She stood up while the others begged her to stay, but she slung her bag over her shoulder, shook her head, and left.

"That's my cue," Deacon said on a sigh, heaving himself up from the couch, "I would be in trouble if I didn't go after her. I'll see you guys later."

Biting my lip, I looked down at the piece of treat left in my hand. The idea of eating it curdled my stomach.

"Well, I screwed that all up. Sorry guys," I said, getting up from the couch, my knee twinging and getting stuck halfway up.

Forcing my knee to extend the rest of the way when it got stuck was supposedly something to avoid, but my physical therapist and my surgeon weren't there. And it happened at least once a day no matter how hard I tried to follow the rest of their guidance.

Olivia winced as she watched the hitch in my process of

standing, but neither her nor Campbell made a move to stop me from leaving. They just sat there looking dejected.

Our group night at karaoke was a disaster.

But damned if I could figure out any other way it was going to work out.

Something was going on with Katie, Deacon was stuck trying to deal with it, Olivia and Campbell got lost in the shuffle, and I was not in a position to help any of them.

Next time one of my friends suggested a get together, I would do them all a favor and stay home with my knee up.

"Hey, Theresa," Olivia said, turning to look at me as I opened the door to the private little karaoke room.

"Don't worry. I'll be there in the morning," I said, before I walked out through the lobby. Rain pelted the windows outside, coming in sideways on a stiff wind.

Great, limping my way to the truck and pulling myself up into it was already a chore. In the rain it felt like a cruel joke on me in particular.

The sound of the wind, rain, and cars speeding past the parking lot on the street splashing water all around them, was louder and more discordant than even my singing would have been. But this was the only song I was going to get tonight.

Once I hauled myself into the truck and shut the door behind me, I pulled my phone out of my coat pocket to make sure it wasn't too wet.

It was dry, but it also showed I had a message from Samantha.

After almost a year.

After no contact for over ten months since she walked out of my hospital room crying, I didn't care what she had to say now.

Eventually I might try dating again, but just seeing her name was enough for me to never again want to put myself in the position of loving someone enough that if it didn't work out it would crush me.

I dropped my phone into the cup holder of the truck and grabbed my braced knee, situating it more comfortably to the side of the pedals before starting it up and pulling out of the parking lot.

There was no great way for my leg to sit while in the truck, and I still had to climb the steps to my room in my mom's house when I got home. It made me tired just thinking about it.

Life made me tired at the moment.

My mom would say I was being self-pitying, but so what if I was?

I had to move back in with her, work for her, drive a company vehicle, and pretend I wasn't crushed that all my plans and dreams for my future were as torn apart as my knee?

Yeah, that wasn't going to happen.

What was going to happen was ice, jammies, and sleep before I had to wake up too damn early to hobble my way to Pike Place and help Olivia's friend.

At least I might get a cinnamon roll out of the deal and then go home to sleep.

Now that sounded like a life plan.

Cinnamon rolls and naps.

But I had no idea how to make that my reality instead of this constant pain in my knee, the giant stupid truck, and a job that didn't quite fit.

CEECEE

*N*othing fit, or at least it didn't fit comfortably.

I threw my stupid dress back into my bag of clothes and decided that it was Saturday, so it didn't matter what I wore.

My mom would have been pissed at me for not even trying to wear something business appropriate, but I no longer cared. Something had to give. I had to stop worrying about all the ways I needed to be and all the things I needed to do for my mom until I took care of the most important thing. Until that was done, none of the rest of it mattered anyway.

Even if I could still shove my thighs into something, or button a shirt over my stomach and my boobs, it wasn't like I could afford the cost of dry cleaning anyway. My nicest clothes taunted me from the box they were packed in. A box I should have dropped off in the covered area outside the shelter where I hauled a bunch of my other things to. But I just couldn't let go of them. Not yet.

Even after staying up far too late taking care of things and bustling my world around the city, I still had to leave behind my couch and my dresser. I couldn't carry them by myself.

And no one knew what I did.

What had to be done.

I couldn't let them.

Stress might not kill me—even though it felt like it might as I stared into my bag of limited options—but it was certain death to my wardrobe.

The timer on the oven sounded and I threw on an old t-shirt over my leggings. I was out of time to worry about my stupid clothes.

My racks of trays were filled with the treats and goods for the day. The last of my trays were going to have to go directly to the cases out front. That was fine. They were all full of cinnamon rolls anyway.

Of all the items we sold, making extra cinnamon rolls was always a good idea, and I needed the money.

A random idea popped into my head. I thought had the potential to sell as well as the cinnamon rolls. This time it was maple cinnamon rolls. But coming up with an idea I thought had potential, like lemon zucchini bread with glaze on top, or the blueberry ricotta rolls, wasn't the problem. The problem was the time, resources, and money it would take to make it work. I had to work with what I had that sold, even though the ideas kept on coming. And it had been happening for months.

But just like every time before, I shoved it aside and focused on the giant list I needed to complete that was already sitting in front of me.

Glancing up at the clock on the wall, I tried to guess how much time it would take me to finish, but I was too tired.

Running on three hours of sleep was not working for my brain.

All I knew was that I had twenty-seven minutes until we opened. It was going to be close. And I needed to shut down early because there was no way I was going to be able to make it to closing.

If we did everything right, there might be time for Marcus to run next door and pick us up some coffees.

My kitchen was a mess. All of the ingredients that needed to be kept cold were packed in ice in every cooler I was able to get my hands on—which meant piles of coolers in every corner of the kitchen.

Hopefully, Olivia's friend would be here soon to help with the situation, but the refrigerator was ancient. I didn't have much hope.

Taking the cinnamon rolls out of the oven, I took a deep breath full of their perfect balance of spice and sweet before drowning them in icing.

Everyone loved the rolls once the icing was thick on top and dripping down the sides, while I preferred them right before that. Hot, fluffy, and full of flavor.

But I couldn't take the time to eat one, not when I still had so much to do before I opened.

A knock sounded on the front door, and I cursed under my breath.

Of course, someone would come early today when I was still scrambling.

Instead of answering it, I bustled around the kitchen, finishing the last-minute items on my list before I started to transfer everything to the front cases.

I had no idea when I was going to get a chance to clean up all the dishes, the trays, the counters, the ovens, and the floors, and not be so exhausted I wanted to curl up in a corner and pass out. I had very little hope of that moment coming anytime soon.

As it was, I was for sure going to need to wake up early tomorrow to head to the Y to take a shower. It was already too much to add another time-consuming task to the morning work I was putting off until tomorrow.

I muttered more curse words, hoping my mother wasn't a ghost and therefore couldn't hear me.

When, exactly, was I supposed to fix the toilet? When was I supposed to go get groceries? Where was I going to put the groceries if Olivia's friend wasn't able to fix the fridge?

The back door opened and Marcus came in, bringing with him the rain and a chill wind that cooled off the hair along the nape of my neck where I was starting to sweat from so much hurrying.

"Get in here. Someone is already at the front door," I said over my shoulder as I ran past him and placed the last of the cinnamon rolls in the case.

"Alright, alright. Jeez, keep your pants on…" His voice cut off suddenly and I turned around to see what the issue was.

He stood in the hall with his apron still not tied and his head cocked to the side with one eyebrow high.

I looked around me and couldn't spot what the issue was.

"Sweetie, did you put your makeup on in the dark?" he asked.

"Oh, crap." I deflated, because yes, I had. I was still half asleep and didn't want to clutter up the bathroom because he couldn't know where I was living now. "What did I do?"

Biting his lips and trying to suppress a laugh, he said, "You used purple lip liner as brow pencil."

"Ahhh! Oh lord." I pulled off my gloves, suppressing further screams, and ran into the bathroom, scrubbing my face of the ridiculous color. It only partially worked.

I darted from the bathroom to the office, shutting the door behind me and dragging in a deep breath before I grabbed my makeup bag and tried to fix my face. No matter what I did, my eyebrows still had a more reddish cast to them than normal.

"Damn it," I said to the empty room. There wasn't time for me to do anything else. I was just going to have to look mildly ridiculous for the rest of the day.

Rushing out of the office, slamming the door behind me again, I skipped going to the front and went directly to the kitchen, getting more trays to put into the cases.

But the trays weren't all I had to do. I needed to find an apron before I opened the door.

"Where are all the aprons?" I called, running back to the kitchen after dropping off the trays for Marcus to take care of.

"They're in the bin by the door. I washed them all last night. Why are you running? We still have twenty minutes," Marcus said, his normally perfect looks marred by the fact that his face was screwed up to the side like he was starting to worry about me.

"Can you get the door please?" I didn't wait for him to answer, just headed to the aprons and started to don mine. The people who came before we opened might have been irritating, but they were some of our best customers. I didn't want to piss one of them off.

I snapped the apron string trying to yank it back around to my front too fast.

"Damn it," I muttered. I meant to drape it over the side of the bin but wasn't paying close enough attention and it slipped to the floor.

Bending over and trying to snag it out from under the bench the bin rested on, I heard Marcus open the front door and the low tones of him talking quietly with someone while I kept grumbling.

Finally, my hand closed over the fabric of the apron, and I pulled it out as I stood up.

Too fast. I stood up too fast after bending over and not enough sleep.

Someone stood in front of me, but it was impossible to tell if it was Marcus or not.

The edges of my vision shrank inward, narrowing my wobbly view, and then all I could see was the ceiling.

THERESA

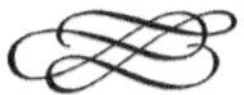

I was soaked, cold, and my knee was already screaming. Damn good start to the day, limping my way down the hill into Pike Place Market to get here with my toolbox and tool belt weighing me down. Olivia owed me huge.

Marcus, the guy who let me in the door, was yammering on about something to do with opening and that I really needed to talk to Ceecee.

"So, where is Ceecee?" I asked, aiming for jovial and winding up sounding closer to surly. Which…was probably more accurate anyway.

"Right back there. Walk on through," he said, starting to fuss with the signage at the front and a little table and chairs to the side.

Okay, I guess that was all the direction I was going to get.

I walked back around the glass-fronted cases filled to bursting with heavenly smells and items that made my mouth water.

Until I spotted some of the same treats I was eating with my friends the night before.

All my interest in gorging myself flew right out of my head chased by memories of a messed-up time that should have been fun.

Focus, Theresa.

I was there to do a job, and when I was done, I could go back to relaxing for the weekend.

No one was behind the counter, but in a hallway toward the back, a girl was bent over messing with something on the floor.

Her butt was perfectly heart shaped in a pair of stretch pants and an oversized T-shirt draped down that blocked her face.

Don't stare. Don't ogle.

Oh, it was hard not to.

The girl whipped up with a wad of fabric in her hand and whirled around to face me.

Her cheeks up to her hairline were red, her mouth partially open, and her eyes rolled back into her head before she started to topple.

Lurching forward, I tried to grab for her. My knee brace caught, stopping me from twisting it wrong, but it sent me falling on my ass.

The girl landed with her head in my lap, blinking at the ceiling.

"Are you okay?" I asked through gritted teeth, the place where the knee brace strapped against my thigh felt like a terrible rug burn and my tailbone was pissed off.

"No. That sucked," she said, her voice sweet and plaintive, with a melodic quality to it that made me assume she was a far better singer than me.

"You didn't hit your head, but are you sick? Is that why you passed out?" I asked. At the same time, Marcus skidded to a stop on his knees in front of us.

"Ceecee, we've talked about this. You have to eat in the

morning." He took her hands and helped haul her to her feet, leaving me to grab onto the wall to lever myself up with one leg.

My brace never let me bend that knee far enough for it to help me in moments like this.

"I'm so sorry. I'm Ceecee. Let me get you something on the house for helping," she said, her voice breathless and rushed.

"No, that's okay." I turned around and looked at her. The color in her face returned to a less tomatoey shade.

She was so pretty that I froze.

This girl had the kind of smile that should have been on a toothpaste commercial and the kind of lips that should have been modeling lipstick, full and a perfect cupid's bow.

"Um," Mason said, looking between us, "Ceecee, this is Theresa. She's here to fix stuff."

Well, that was not very specific. And it made her stand up straighter and eye me with distrust.

"Oh, you're Olivia's," she said.

"Nope." I was a lot of things, but not Olivia's. She looked even more suspicious. "I'm just her friend who happens to be a contractor. Campbell is hers."

I left out that once upon a time her statement was true, but it had not been that way for a while. And the last person who could have called me their anything other than family or friend didn't want to be tied down to someone who washed out. Her words, not mine.

"Are you going to be okay doing this work with your knee in that brace?" she asked, dropping the bundle of fabric in her hand onto a bench and grabbing another from a bin that looked just like it.

"Yeah, well, until it heals as good as it can, I don't really have a choice." My voice was more caustic than I intended, but too damn many people were starting to treat me like I was incapable of anything now that I was no longer able to do what I had always wanted.

Sure, I didn't know what I was going to do now, long term, but I was still able to do *something*. I was already doing something, right at that second, and that something was thinking about walking out.

"Okay," she said, tying a pink apron with a ridiculous white lace ruffle around her waist. Her name was embroidered on one corner and it said, 'The Bake Place' in the center. It looked like the frillier version of the aprons from Olivia's restaurant. "Well, come on back here, and I'll show you the problem."

I trailed after her into a kitchen that looked like it doubled as a camping store stock room for all the coolers stacked in the corners.

"Right here is the fridge." She opened the door of one of the oldest commercial refrigerators I had ever seen still in use.

We had a few clients that were businesses in the area—some of whom had been around for years—but this fridge might have been older than those businesses were.

"Do you have any guesses on what the problem is?" I bent to get a look into the dials on the inside of the fridge just to check they were set properly. They looked fine, so that wasn't the problem.

"No, not what caused it anyway. It keeps making sounds like it's running, but it isn't cooling at all." She wrung the end of the apron between her hands like she was trying to strangle it.

"Let me pull it out from the wall and see what I can find out. Is this the only thing? Because with an appliance of this age it might be better just to replace it. Often if something starts breaking when it's this old, other things will soon follow." I started to shove at the back of the hurking thing, slow-walking it out one side at a time from the wall.

Ceecee didn't answer me, and I glanced at her only to see her mouth set in a line and her eyebrows drawn together.

Although I had no idea what I did that pissed her off, she clearly was. So I just focused on what I was doing.

Which was a damn favor. One that seemed a lot less small at the moment.

I couldn't watch this anymore. I was likely to tell Theresa to get out of here any minute, and it wasn't even her fault.

Not entirely anyway.

She didn't know about my financial situation.

How could she possibly know that to suggest something as simple as replacing the fridge would force me to resort to being angry to keep from crying?

This whole day was going to be hard. I still wasn't sure how I was going to explain that I also needed her to fix the pipe in the bathroom. And every second she was there, I feared the owner showing up, her notifying him, someone from the Board of Health coming in, something else breaking, and most of all at that second: The bill.

Some Saturday.

While she worked, I grabbed a blueberry muffin and went to the office.

Back here, behind the shut door, I stole a few moments to

eat something and get a drink from the water bottle on my desk.

The whole time, I tried not to think.

Not about all the things scaring me so much I had nightmares in the few hours of sleep I did manage to get. And not about the fact that Theresa looked a lot like the cheerleader I had a crush on in high school who treated me like crap the first time I got up the nerve to talk to her because I was a fat girl.

In high school, her name was Vanessa and she had red hair with a smattering of freckles across her nose. But that nose was a tiny turned-up thing like Theresa's and her eyes were also blue like Theresa's.

Theresa had blonde hair and her eyes were lighter blue, almost grey. But she had that same perfect body with the athletic build of someone who spent a lot of time working out. Although, she also had the tool belt and work clothes that gave her a Rosie the Riveter vibe that only managed to make her more intimidating.

She may have been Olivia's friend, but my whole body wanted to turn her away and never talk to her again.

Even though I thought girls like her were beautiful, I knew I would never have a chance with one. To try would only end in terrible disappointment and heartbreak.

"Ceecee, what all is she here to do?" Marcus asked, wiggling his eyebrows up and down at me as I came back into the front of the store.

"Stop it. We need some things worked on, that's all. Don't get weird." I shook my head as the chime above the door announced someone coming in.

We worked hard enough in the first hour that I managed to put what was happening in the kitchen out of my mind.

"Do you think there will be a lull enough for me to pop next door and get us coffees?" he asked, moving past me with a box loaded with treats for one of our customers headed to their office. Because I wasn't the only small business owner who didn't take weekends.

"Probably, but first I need to check on her and let her know about the other thing." I didn't want to tell the customers about all the broken and held-together parts of the bakery.

Maybe they wouldn't trust the food, or maybe they would turn me in to the health department or the building owner if they knew we didn't have a working toilet.

At least the sink was still functioning. If that broke it would be a disaster.

When the lull finally came, Marcus tapped me on the shoulder and gestured to the kitchen.

I blew out a breath, puffing away the short tendrils of hair that had fallen from my messy top knot.

"Go, before we get slammed again so I can get us coffee," he said, rubbing his hands together and looking like he was going to lick the counter in front of him he was so thirsty.

"You are ridiculous. Fine," I said, smiling and shaking my head. At least his antics made me slightly less nervous to talk to her.

In the kitchen, Theresa was shoving the fridge back into place, adjusting the brace on her knee every time she went from one side to the other in a crab-walking kind of maneuver.

"How is it going back here?" I asked, cringing at how stilted I sounded. It was like I was reading from the world's worst script.

"Well, do you want," she grunted, shoving the last bit on one side to get it nestled in place, "the good news or the bad news?"

If I was reading from a terrible script, at least she was too.

"Bad news," I said, although I didn't want it at all. In my head I said goodbye to the money Mrs. Williams had given me and the headstone I planned on buying for my mother with it.

"This thing is not going to last for more than a year or two. I fixed it. You can use it again. But prepare to replace it soon."

Somewhere in me I knew this was coming, but I was so happy it was a year or two away and not right that second. I flung my arms around her neck and hugged her.

Theresa went rigid in my grip, and I stepped back, laughing and trying to pretend this didn't just reach high levels of awkward.

"I'm sorry, I know that's not great and I'm working with borrowed time and now I have to budget for that, but you bought me a year before I need to worry about it. So, thank you."

Her face was rigid. I couldn't tell if she was scared or angry, or what was going on in her head. But even her bad news had not been as bad as what I was expecting.

"Can I show you the other thing I need fixed?" My words came out so fast they flowed together, and I wasn't sure she understood me until she nodded.

"Okay, so I think it's a leak in the water pipe supplying the toilet. I have the main turned on right now, but other than for washing our hands, I haven't had it on since I discovered the problem yesterday."

We walked out of the kitchen and through the front door. I spotted one of the neighbors who lived in the apartments upstairs reaching for the handle.

If they spotted Theresa here, there would be trouble. What if they told the owner? Would I be able to say it was just the fridge and I fixed it so he couldn't shut me down?

There were too many questions, too many risks, and not even close to enough chance that it wouldn't end in absolute disaster.

I shuffled to the side and let Theresa get ahead of me in the doorway to the bathroom before I shoved her the rest of the way in the door.

She stumbled and grunted, catching herself before she fell over.

Taking a swift breath of relief, I said, "I have to take care of something really quick. I'll be right back."

Catching a glimpse of her face—which looked like a mask of sheer betrayal—I whirled around to the front and met the neighbor at the glass case as she bent to peer into it.

"Hi, Ceecee," she said, lifting a hand above her head, her gaze fixed on one of the cinnamon rolls.

"Good morning. Can I get you one?" I asked, trying to catch my breath.

Every time I had a run-in with one of my neighbors or my landlord, my chest got tight and it grew hard to breathe. I would have preferred to be as friendly with them as I used to be, but now it felt like if I stepped wrong, I would fall over.

"Yes, that would be great. I need to get them while I can," she said.

"What do you mean?" I bent over and started to box up her cinnamon roll, expecting something about a vacation or a new job where she would be going in early.

"Has no one told you?" She furrowed her brow and the corners of her mouth turned down. Her chin quivered.

If I didn't know better, I would have assumed she was going to cry.

"No, I thought you knew. Most of us are moving out." She gestured with a halfhearted wave to the rest of the building above me where four apartments were.

"But why? And most of us?" I couldn't make sense out of her words.

"The rent is going up again. Most of us can't afford it anymore. But while I'm still here, I want to get more of these perfect cinnamon rolls." She smiled at me and took the box out of my hands, leaving behind the money for it.

I didn't know what to say. There weren't words for this.

Of course, I was aware of the landlord raising the rents. He wanted to do the same to me, but he couldn't. He was trapped by the contract he signed with my mom all those years ago. It was the whole reason I couldn't afford to give him an excuse to put me out.

But this?

I wasn't expecting him to push the upstairs tenants so hard, upping their rents so much and so often that he would force them out.

"What is he thinking?" I mumbled, turning around and spotting Theresa standing near the end of the hallway with a piece of pipe in her hand.

She couldn't afford me.

Maybe she got something different out of the conversation she just had, but I knew that look.

There was desperation in her face. The same kind I saw on the faces of the clients we sometimes got that only wanted a band aid fix when what they needed was a lot more involved, and therefore a lot more expensive.

Now I understood the hug in the kitchen.

She couldn't afford the fridge replacement, and she wouldn't be able to afford what really needed fixed in the bathroom.

Although she should have been able to call her terrible landlord who kept increasing the rent. If she was having trouble paying what he expected her to, then she should have been calling on him to do his part and fix the issues in the old building.

"Hey, sorry about that, let me see how it's going," she said, walking with me toward the bathroom.

"No need. I know what I have to do, and it's simple really.

But I need some parts," I said, holding up the piece in my hand. Although that wasn't the whole truth.

"Oh, okay, well we'll be here all day, so after you get the parts will you be coming back?" Ceecee asked, her eyes blinking too much and her brows high like she was trying to fight off tears.

"Yes, I'll be back today." I nodded and turned to walk out, not understanding the twisting in my gut at the thought of her crying.

I wanted to fix all of it for her even though I barely knew her.

The hug in the kitchen was the first time someone who wasn't a friend of mine had hugged me since my knee blew out.

Maybe that was why I suddenly felt like I needed to help. Maybe all it took for me to get attached was a little bit of contact.

Ceecee and Marcus were talking about coffee as I walked out the front door.

But I had some planning to do. The first step of which was heading to the shop and getting some supplies. I wasn't lying about that.

The second step...I wasn't sure of yet.

Although I had a decent idea of where to start.

My knee started to scream at me while making my way up the hill to where I parked the truck. The patch of skin that was rubbed raw in the fall with Ceecee made me want to take a detour and bandage my leg.

It also made me swear under my breath as I realized it was Saturday and I was about to willfully give up an okay parking spot as far as Pike Place parking went. I would likely be screwed trying to find another.

Some things—no matter how crappy and how much I didn't want to deal with them— couldn't be helped.

By the time I made it to the truck and hauled myself into it, I had to sit with my legs dangling out the open door for a minute and rest my head against the seat.

Up and down my leg the muscles ached, the bones felt weak like noodles, and the ligaments in my knee—the real problem—felt like they wanted to snap in half again.

"Please let me get through today. I will baby you tomorrow," I said out loud to my knee.

I pulled out my phone and texted Olivia.

What do you know about The Bake Place?

She was quick to respond which meant that Joe's probably wasn't open yet.

Ceecee's mom passed away not that long ago and now she runs it by herself.

Well, that was interesting, but it didn't tell me much more than I already knew. And it certainly didn't explain exactly what was going on.

How long has it been there? That's pretty prime retail space.

Normally anyway. Right at that moment it was the opposite.

Any time major construction went on in one area of the city, there was some fallout for the businesses because traffic was already challenging around Seattle. During construction? Most people didn't want to have anything to do with the area being worked on.

It's been there forever. I think Ceecee basically grew up in that bakery.

In some ways, Ceecee was so much like Olivia it was scary.

For a second, I froze, staring down at my phone and wondering why I wanted to help this girl so bad.

Yes, I thought she was gorgeous. Yes, I thought the bakery was something that should continue. And yes, it seemed to matter to my friends a lot.

But it wasn't as if a girl like Ceecee would ever want to date someone like me. She might not even want to be friends with me.

She was like Samantha and Olivia—someone who knew exactly what they wanted out of life. They were also the kind of people who didn't just know what they wanted. They were going after it. Active in pursuit of their dreams.

I, on the other hand, was going through the motions.

The moment in my hospital room with Sam ran through my head, the moment when she said she couldn't be with someone who washed out, someone who didn't have direction and had no idea what they were going to do.

Dropping my head back against the headrest and swinging my legs into the truck, I lamented my choices. All these amazing girls, I couldn't help but be attracted to them for their passion and their drive.

Meanwhile, I was no longer one of them, and I couldn't imagine any relationship with someone like them would end any differently for me than my relationship with Sam had ended.

First, I pushed Olivia away because she was too much for me, and I thought I would be going away to college for cheer while she would never leave Seattle or her family's restaurant.

Then, I went and trashed my knee and lost Sam in the process too.

Now what?

Continue to get to know Ceecee and risk falling for her before I knew what I wanted out of my life and what, if anything, I could offer her?

I shut the door and started the truck. Making my way out of the parking spot and out of the Pike Place area, I headed toward the shop and the first of what I was increasingly coming to believe would be a series of mistakes.

Because no matter how hard I tried to talk myself out of it, I wanted to help Ceecee.

Maybe if I helped her keep her dream, I would be putting out good vibes that would oddly let me find my own dream.

"She's cute," Marcus said, wiggling his eyebrows at me as he handed me a coffee.

I rolled my eyes and took a sip, the heat and sugar managing to give me just enough of a boost to delusionally believe I could make it through the rest of the day.

"Come on. Work with me here. I know you noticed." His voice was thick with innuendo, and I wanted to smack him for it as warmth spread up my face.

"Yeah, well, she's not exactly my type," I said.

He snorted.

"Shut up, you. How would you even know. You think girls are yucky." I shook my head as he grinned over his cup at me. "Besides, I have too much to do around here to think about dating. Let alone think about dating a girl like her."

"Girl like her…" He narrowed his eyes at me and then shook his head. "Nope. I'm going to start with the first point you think you made and work my way up to that one."

I walked away from him to restock the bags.

Please, someone, anyone, come in and save me.

"For me, yes, girls are yucky. Beyond the ones I love completely." He stuck his nose in the air and I couldn't help but smile.

Being one of those that he loved completely was one of the highlights of my life.

"However," he said.

Oh, now he was going to remind me why that complete love was also a royal pain in the butt.

"I am not blind, Ceecee. I am gay. There is a difference. And even a blind person would be able to see that Theresa is super hot." He fanned himself with a hand and it was everything I could do to avoid rewarding his ridiculous behavior with a laugh.

"And you know it. You also know that it is not healthy to limit your entire life to this place and me. While I am great company, and our love is beyond whatever may come from a girlfriend for you and boyfriend for me, we are sadly lacking the very nature the other most desires."

Standing up and turning to look at him, I lost it. My laugh was loud and long, made more so by the utter lack of shame on his face.

"Don't pretend to be innocent now, Marcus." I rolled my eyes and wiped under them, hoping the giggle tears leaking out wouldn't leave me with mascara runs to match my already botched eyebrows.

"Fine." He waved a hand at me, his face breaking into a smile. "But I made my point. You need to let yourself have a chance. Go on a date. Do it for me, because we both know I will perpetually hide behind my love for you to avoid putting myself out there."

I made my way to him, leaned my head on his shoulder, and looked out the windows at the rain sheeting down outside.

He wrapped an arm around my back and leaned his head on mine.

I knew the real reason why he was closed off to romance. I was there for the entire thing, including the desperate search and the days he spent drowning in tears.

"But she's…way out of my league." I whispered.

Marcus stiffened next to me and pulled his head off mine.

It didn't matter that I couldn't see him, I felt his eyes boring holes into the top of my head.

"Ceecee." His voice was missing all the playfulness it usually held.

He was mad so rarely, that I couldn't help but look up at him.

"Don't you ever say that again. You are amazing. And beautiful. Even when you screw up your makeup. Stop it."

While I didn't believe him, I nodded anyway.

"Okay, so now that we've gone through your valley of nuttiness, are you going to ask this girl out or do I have to do it for you?"

And I was laughing again.

"Like my own Cyrano de Bergerac?"

"Eeek, no." He shook his head and looked like I just held a slug under his nose.

I laughed as the chime above the door sounded and a whoosh of cold air and dampness flowed into the bakery.

Marcus turned to help the customer and I made my way to the kitchen, tucking my coffee on the shelf by the door after another sip to strengthen me.

Standing on the threshold of the kitchen, staring down the utter disaster it had become, there wasn't enough coffee in the world to stave off the deep urge rising within me to cry and beg for my mom.

But, with a sniff, I resisted the flood of need, grabbed

another tray, and headed back out to the front to reload the cases.

The customer was already walking out, a large box in one arm.

"You were fast with that one," I said, loading up one of the cases.

"It was cookies and cash. It only takes a minute. She comes in all the time for a box of cookies for her work and got some for home this time. But she knows exactly how much they cost." Marcus grabbed his coffee and perched himself on one of the tall stools along the wall behind the counter.

"Or, instead of sitting there, you could maybe help me restock?" I muttered at the tray in my hand, adjusting my hold in the automatic way I always did as I emptied it into the case that was only half in need of the buns that I loaded it with.

"Or you could just wait until we actually need to slide out a whole empty tray and can just slide in a full one," he said, his voice the same tone as mine, but a whole lot louder.

"Mom always said that if you wait to sell the last roll, it will end up on your dinner plate." I smiled to myself and sniffed again. For some reason, that small memory of my mom tickled the back of my eyes, threatening me with tears I didn't want to shed anymore. At least not today.

"Ceecee," he said from behind me, his voice soft and all the joviality leeched out of it, "You need a break. Let me do that. And why don't you spend some time in the kitchen or the office or something."

I shook my head, straightening with my now half-empty tray.

"Work helps," I said, and I turned away from him to head to the kitchen. But I saw it on his face.

He knew that was lie.

Maybe work used to help.

Actually, it wasn't a maybe. It did help in the direct aftermath of losing Mom. But now, work was the source of all the stress. And it didn't matter.

Because whether it helped or not, it was all I had.

The tray went back to its place, and I made my way through all the coolers to check that the ice wasn't melting too fast before I got everything loaded back into the fridge.

Of course, all of it was melting.

Really, there was no other option.

"Please help, Theresa," I said to the empty room.

She was pretty much my only hope to fix this whole mess.

"*D*amn it, Seattle," I grumbled, stepping carefully along the cobblestones on Pike Place.

I loved my city, but the parking down here was a disaster. The stupid construction made it so much worse.

The hike down the hill with my bags of stuff made me question my own commitment to this ridiculous mission to save the bakery.

But Olivia was probably spreading the word among our friends, and they might kill me if I was part of the reason that they couldn't get their cinnamon rolls.

Damn it.

My knee was going to be pissed off at me by the end of the day for sure.

If I didn't get this project done today, I wasn't sure I was going to be able to get back down this hill again tomorrow.

I ran through all the possible ways I could pack the truck so I wouldn't have to fight for parking space and could get here in the ridiculous early morning hours again.

Checklists. That was the only answer. Checklists of stuff that

I could shove into every toolbox in the truck for any eventuality was the only way to park in the morning and not have to move again.

Even with that, the prospect of going back and forth all day hauling stuff was exhausting just to think about.

And I hated checklists.

Of all the things I missed about college, checklists weren't among them.

I could keep the myriad things I needed to do for work straight in my head without them. But for some reason, I never could keep straight the schedules of all my assignments and classes while I was in school.

Despite the rain, people poured past me with their hoods up and their faces pointed down at the ground, picking their way carefully through the puddles in the grayness.

The lone umbrella in the crowd had a couple huddled underneath it. They looked lost, their heads turning from side to side and pointing in opposite directions.

Even if the umbrella wasn't the biggest tell, their confusion marked them as tourists.

I sighed.

Most likely I was about to get even more soaked and be waylaid for longer than I wanted while my knee screamed. My arms started to ache from the weight of my bags. But I couldn't let them remain lost.

Like most cities, mine could be difficult to navigate once someone was lost. Especially since they were likely to confuse Pike and Pine or the streets that repeated north and south. Not to mention the one-ways. No one enjoyed getting turned around by one of those.

"Hey, do you need directions? You look a little lost," I said, coming up to their side.

Did they answer? No. But they twirled to face me, sending a

spray of water flinging off the umbrella's edge directly into my face.

"Oh, I'm so sorry," one of them said as I blinked the water out of my eyes and adjusted the bags to reach up and wipe my face.

"No big deal. Can I help you find something?" I asked, trying to keep a friendly tone in my voice even though I think I only managed to stay neutral. Better than coming off as a grumpy Seattleite like we were usually painted.

"That would be so great. You know the area?"

It was everything I could do not to say something snarky. I was in the pouring rain, loaded with bags of tools and parts, my tool belt weighing down my waist, my work clothes on, and a knee brace.

What, exactly, about any of that made it seem like I was on a touristy walkabout of the city?

"Yeah, lived here all my life," I said, instead of asking if they lost their brain when they lost their way.

"Oh, you are a life saver. Do you know where The Bake Place is? We are supposed to be meeting someone there."

I almost laughed out loud, but just nodded and smiled.

They did a collective little jig and juggle of their umbrella, managing to slosh me with water again as I took off in the direction we needed to go.

"So, where are you from?" I asked, ducking my head down again, even though any semblance of makeup and level of put together had to be totally gone by then.

"Maybe we're from Tacoma," one of them said, their voice jovial.

First, they just named the only other city in Washington many people knew of. Second, no one from this state carried an umbrella even if they didn't know Seattle itself. Third, chances were a Washingtonian who was lost in downtown would have asked that question with 'East of the mountains' as their example.

I shook my head and smiled.

"Just a feeling," I said.

"We're from Arizona, outside of Phoenix in Scottsdale."

"You went the wrong direction, didn't you?" I asked, while they looked even more confused. "Don't you sunbirds usually come here in the summer?"

"Usually," one of them laughed, their giggle high and a little too tight. "But we have some business opportunities to handle that couldn't be done over the phone."

People were often a little tight-lipped about business opportunities, but these two were being even cagier than most people I knew. And I knew a bunch of foodies who guarded their foodie secrets with their fangs out first.

"Oh, so you're international spies. Good to know. I'll watch myself."

Cutting my eyes sideways at them, I watched as it took a moment for them to realize I was kidding.

When they did, they decided I was hilarious, laughing wildly.

In the process, they dumped the rain off their umbrella all over me.

So, all in all, it was decidedly not worth the joke.

But it was either that or they were in porn. I was going with porn. Katie would love this story, while Deacon would want to hide under a table at the mention of the word.

The Bake Place's sign finally peeked at me through the downpour, and I hitched the bag more securely up my shoulder.

A car had somehow made its way through the construction and didn't seem to realize they were blocking the narrow lane by parking in what was actually the middle of the road.

Pike Place was a confusing mix of walking open market and

narrow street, sure, but this person really needed someone to explain how it all worked before they got towed.

My companions got excited and got ahead of me when they spotted the sign.

At least I wouldn't have to juggle my bags to open the door.

I had to appreciate the small benefits of a good deed.

Even if it was performed in service to international spies who really needed Google Maps.

CEECEE

Today wasn't going to end up being a bad sales day. That was a big win.

It didn't stop me from running the figures through my head, and trying to figure out if I was going to have enough money to cover the cost of paying Theresa for the repairs.

Not surprisingly, it wasn't. But knowing that didn't stop me from trying to dream up ways I could make it become a trend large enough to offset the months of construction-caused downturn in profits.

Lost in my daydreams, I missed the chime above the door while my back was turned so I could straighten the takeout boxes.

"Sir, good afternoon," Marcus said, his voice louder than was necessary, the muscles in my whole body tightening in response.

Who would he call 'sir?'

I turned around with a wide smile plastered on my face. My heart dropped out of my body and ran to hide among the mess in the kitchen. The hello I meant to say lodged in my throat.

"Ceecee," Mr. McCarthy said, giving barely a nod to Marcus. He narrowed his eyes at me, making them look like upside down triangles.

My landlord looked soft, rounded at the edges with a weak chin and the beginnings of jowls. But I knew better than to believe his looks.

"Hi, Mr. McCarthy, what brings you in today?" I spoke too fast and took a deep breath, reminding myself to slow down. I couldn't afford to give the man any excuses to stay any longer than absolutely necessary.

"Well, Ceecee, I was wondering if you heard about what was happening upstairs." He leaned down and perused the things in the cases, pretending that he didn't just hand me a live grenade with the pin pulled.

"No, I haven't heard much, we've been busy this morning." That should help my case…pretend it wasn't something I found out already. "Is it something I should know about for business? You remodeling?"

He laughed. He actually laughed at that. Like the idea of ever willingly improving anything about the building was so absurd it was comical.

This man…But instead of saying anything, I ground my teeth and kept the smile on my face.

Pretending to know nothing was always the best strategy when it came to him.

"Actually, some of the neighbors are changing upstairs." He glanced up at me, looking for it to register on my face, I was sure.

So I feigned shock.

"Oh, that's too bad. I like the neighbors. They are good people." The neighbors he was running out of the homes they had been in forever and whose names he probably had to check before he called them to tell them.

"Yes, well, rents are going up all over the city, and once the construction here is done, this area will get a big boost."

No one could say that for sure. It's what businesses all around me hoped for, but none of us were blessed with clairvoyance. Neither was Mr. McCarthy.

But greed made people guess at all kinds of things. Besides, he didn't want my opinion on what he expected or on rents.

He definitely didn't want my opinion on rent.

"Do you have people already lined up, then?"

There, that was probably neutral enough.

"Can I have one of these?" he asked, artfully dodging my question.

"Of course," I said, grabbing a bag while the chime above the door sounded. I turned around in time to see Theresa walk in with two other people who struggled to manage their umbrella.

Go back outside, I wanted to yell. But instead, I just bent over and bagged his chocolate cream roll, pretending Theresa's presence was no big deal.

Maybe he wouldn't ask. Maybe she wouldn't say anything. Maybe I could just act like she was another customer.

Beside me, Marcus darted out to the other side of the counter and headed her off, pulling her to the side and chatting as if they were old friends.

The energy was so weird that the people that came in with her must have thought they walked into the middle of a performance art show.

"Here you go, Mr. McCarthy," I said.

One of the umbrella people got excited and smacked their companion on the arm before running up to Mr. McCarthy and bopping up and down.

"Oh, we found you!" The umbrella person's voice was like a little kid's when they saw a pony for the first time. Never, not once, did I expect someone would be capable of being that excited by my landlord.

"Ah, I'm glad you could make it," he said, as if he knew exactly who they were.

"This is the bakery I was telling you about, but they are busy right now. So I'll just give you the details while we tour upstairs." He took the bag out of my hand and turned around, leading the newcomers toward the front door.

He seemed to be so distracted that he didn't notice that my hand was stuck in the air, my breath stuck in my lungs, and my heart was no longer in regular rhythm.

As soon as the door shut behind the three of them, I yelled, "What did he mean tour? Tour here? In the bakery? Today?"

Marcus ran over to the front window, pressing his face to the glass.

"They're all under the umbrella, looking up at the building. McCarthy is gesturing up and down the street. Now they're headed to the door to the apartments."

His report didn't help.

I was in danger of passing out.

"Someone tell me this isn't what I think it is." My voice sounded like it came from far away.

Which made sense because my mind was heading upstairs with them, trying to figure out how long I had before they would be back, and if it would be enough time to try and hide some of the coolers and all my bags in the office.

"Ceecee, breathe. Maybe he's just showing them one of the apartments upstairs." Marcus turned back to me and patted Theresa on his way past her toward the counter.

As if it was her cue, she started making her way around the counter and to the back.

But was it enough? Was her presence and her work enough to get me out of this?

I brought them in here.

Would Ceecee care that I didn't know what was going on?

My back ached as I dropped all my stuff down. My shoulders yelled so much it took me a minute to stretch everything out before I could even begin to think.

Her landlord was selling the place, that much seemed clear.

Maybe Marcus and Ceecee could tell themselves they were just there to look at renting one of the apartments, but I knew better.

And what would that do to Ceecee's business? If she was having trouble making payments to her landlord now, how would she ever be able to pay for the space once the new people took over?

Because no matter how nice the people seemed — weird but nice — they would increase the rent. That's just the way things worked.

Getting down to the floor took work, although there was no way around it.

Once I was down there and my knee was as comfortable as it was going to get, I started on my work. The concern over Ceecee and her situation still ran through the back of my mind.

"Do you need anything?" Ceecee's voice came from behind me at the door, and I paused to put the last of the tools I just used back into one of the bags.

"Actually, could I get something to eat and drink real quick before I move on to the next step?" No need to explain to her that the next step would make everything look worse before I got it looking better.

"Of course. Come on." She turned and headed toward the front although I expected her to go to the kitchen.

"Crap." The problem with asking for a break and a snack was that I had to get up.

Shoving up from the ground, I got to where I could kick my leg out behind me and use my arms and other leg to lift myself the rest of the way up from leaning on the toilet seat.

At least she wasn't in here to see me look like a fool. But somehow, I needed to get off my knee soon.

Rounding the corner, I almost wound up back on my butt.

Marcus jumped back, his hands flying up into fists like he was going to punch me in the face.

"Geez," I said, a hand to my heart and a smile tugging at me, "I didn't think running into someone was a corporal punishment kind of crime."

He looked at his own hands and burst out laughing as he lowered them back to his sides.

"Sorry. Sometimes when I'm startled my reaction is to fight whatever is coming after me." He shrugged and shook his head. "I don't know why."

Jokes popped into my head. I discarded each of them and nodded instead, stepping aside to let him pass.

We didn't know each other well enough for me to make some of those jokes and say some of those things.

I was well aware that not everyone appreciated my sense of humor.

Marcus continued on to the kitchen and I made my way to the front where Ceecee was putting the lid on a drink from the coffee machine.

"Theresa, I was distracted and didn't ask you how you take your coffee, so I just made you a mocha. I hope that's okay," Ceecee said, looking over her shoulder at me as she finished prepping my drink. She grabbed the box, handing them both off to me.

"Actually, I only like mochas because I don't like coffee. So this is perfect. Thanks." I took a sip and the warmth of the chocolatey drink heated me from the inside out, helping to chase away some of the leftover chill from getting so soaked on my way in. It sent a shiver through me.

"You don't like coffee?" Ceecee asked, tilting her head to the side and looking at me like I just admitted to not liking puppies.

"Not unless it's disguised as chocolate." I held my cup up and did a three-step shuffle to make my way to the little table in the front of the shop.

"Uh, do you mind sitting in the kitchen and eating?" Ceecee chewed on her bottom lip and twisted her apron in her hands.

It didn't matter how nervous she seemed to ask. The question still made me want to help her a lot less. Like I wasn't good enough to sit in the front of the store. I was just the contractor.

I nodded and made my way to where she wanted to hide me, deciding I should just do the most important part of the bigger fix in the bathroom and get out of there.

Trying to be nice, do all that needed done at once, and only charging for the small part seemed like a stupid waste of time if she didn't want me there.

In the kitchen, there was a chair under a tall set of open shelving, like it was normally used as a stool.

Great.

For some reason, the fact that it was a chair no one usually sat in made me feel worse.

But at least the chocolate drink drowned my sorrows some. Opening the box, I found a cinnamon roll.

No appreciation and maybe a wish for me to be gone, but the food was good.

"Small favors," I muttered and took a bite out of the cinnamon roll.

"Hey, can I talk to you really quick?" Marcus whispered from just inside the door as I chewed.

If I had not witnessed his fight response, I would never have guessed the guy in front of me would be capable of it at that moment.

With his hands wrapped around each other, the fingers gripping until the knuckles were white and letting go again, he kept looking over his shoulder.

"Go ahead." I didn't know what else to say to someone who seemed like they were running from a bear.

"Listen, don't tell her this or she will kill me," he said, letting that statement hang in the air. I had no idea how I was supposed to respond so I just sat there for a minute.

Finally, I realized he was waiting for me to acknowledge his out of place comment.

"Sure. I won't say anything."

What in the world could he possibly have to say to me?

"Perfect." He grabbed a stainless-steel stool from under a large island in the mess of a kitchen and pulled it up right across from me. He was so close our knees almost touched.

I raised a brow at him and took another bite. It was better to fill my mouth with food than start saying things out of nerves.

Because I was pretty sure he was team all boys, and him being this in my face made me want to check if I needed to prepare myself to let him down.

Whatever this was, the sooner I was out of this place the better. Because this was weird.

Marcus took a deep breath and said, "I need you to tell me what you think was going on with Mr. McCarthy and his friends."

CEECEE

$\mathcal{M}$arcus always took too long in the kitchen. All he had to do was make another tray of garlic bites.

But I didn't have time to do it for him. We got more customers.

Something about the day—the gloomy rain maybe—seemed to make people need baked goods.

I wasn't complaining.

Whatever the weirdo who didn't like coffee was doing in my bathroom looked complicated, and that usually meant expensive.

Now, if I could just stop worrying about Mr. McCarthy, I would be fine.

"Here you go. Stay dry out there," I said, handing the box to the tourist in their rain jacket with their umbrella tucked under one arm.

The chime above the door jingled as they let themselves out. Olivia scooted in around them, shaking her wet hair out of her face and blinking the water from her eyes like a true Washingtonian.

"I'm surprised to see you here. Don't you usually work today?" I asked by way of hello.

"Yes," she said, the irritation plain in her voice, "But Junior is home and decided to pick up a shift."

Olivia's eyes were wide, her brows high, and her mouth pressed in a grim line.

No matter how hard I tried, I couldn't keep the smile off my face or the laughter from my voice when I asked, "And that's not a good thing?"

"Ugh. Ceecee, if I could just force him never to get near my restaurant again, I would." She shook her head and stomped across the front area to lean on the counter.

"That bad?"

"Whatever you're imagining, it's worse than that. How can he possibly have the time when he's supposed to be in med school?"

"I got nothing," I said and shrugged, which at least got her to smile a little.

"Neither do I. But enough about my brother. I need to ask you for a favor." Her eyes lit up and all the frustration weighing on her face and shoulders fell away.

"You sent me someone who was able to fix my fridge and is fixing the toilet. No favor is too big." I leaned on the counter across from her and put on my biggest smile.

I meant what I said. The thought of trying to find a contractor and a refrigerator repair service made me want to hide. How did anyone hire someone to fix something if they weren't sure they were capable of doing the job right?

Because of Olivia, I knew the person eating in my kitchen was trustworthy.

Plus, she hadn't balked at being asked to hide in case my landlord showed up again.

"Good. Thank you. Because this one might be a pain in the

butt." She looked around at the cases, a line forming between her brows like she was thinking really hard.

What kind of deep thought process could be brought on by baked goods? I just waited while she looked at everything, content to let her decide how I could be of service to her.

"Campbell's aunt, Carmen, is having a birthday on Friday, and I didn't know about it until now. I want to have some cupcakes, or a cake made for her, but I'm not even sure you do that." She looked up at me, hope printed in large letters on her face.

"Yes. I do cakes and cupcakes. Usually only one flavor at a time, but I can make anything. I just don't advertise it because lots of other cupcake and cakes shops are out there." I leaned and pointed to a small cake at the far corner of one of the cases.

"Oh, good." She went to look in on the cake, the smile on her face growing.

"So, normally you do custom cake orders?" She looked back at me. Her smile was so big now that her eyes crinkled at the corners.

"Yes..." For some reason, the giant grin on her face was starting to worry me.

"Perfect. Then, can you make me a cake and some cupcakes, all with different flavors? That way everyone can have their favorite?"

I took a relieved breath, not so scary after all.

"No problem. I do those all the time. How big a cake and how many cupcakes?" I grabbed a pen from the cup on the counter, and the order sheet from just under the edge of the register where it always got tucked away.

Olivia gave me the specifics for a small get together for Carmen's birthday and I took down all the details.

"Have you ever thought about putting up something in here at least to say you do custom work and do at least one more flavor in a day?" she asked, moving back to the one in the case and staring at it with the look of someone who was about to give in and buy something they weren't planning on.

"No. Mom tried it once, and it didn't bring in any additional funds. But the cinnamon rolls…if I could figure out a way to get everyone to want those in the evening too…now that would be great." I laughed and she smiled before she pointed to the case.

"Can I take this one home with me tonight? You know, I need a taste test."

"Ceecee is afraid that if you're out there eating and Mr. McCarthy comes back, he'll remember you and know you've been here too long for you to be a normal customer," Marcus said.

"Oh." That made sense, although it made me feel like a jerk for trying to brush him and his questions off.

"Yeah. So, I thought maybe you had a better idea of what was going on with McCarthy and his little tour. You are involved with real estate."

"Not real estate. I'm a contractor. I fix stuff in houses yeah, but just fix and build stuff." I took another bite of my food and shook my head. He was giving me way too much credit.

"And you work for your mom's company."

It wasn't a question. I wondered if he and Ceecee talked about everything, because I was pretty sure I didn't tell him that.

"How that is relevant, I don't follow, but yes," I said, taking a drink and pretending that he wasn't starting to worry me enough that I was trying to figure out if the cookie sheet next to me would make a decent weapon.

"She's a contractor in this city and she doesn't know realtors or ever flip properties?" He tilted his head and blinked at me.

I relaxed.

"Of course she has. And yes, I get it now. No, I don't even know those people's names. But they asked me for directions, and I thought they were tourists. They did say they were in town for a business opportunity though."

Marcus slumped back in his chair, chewing on his bottom lip and staring just past my shoulder. Every breath seemed to drain something from him, like his will leeched out with each exhale.

"Do you think he's going to sell the building?" he asked, looking back at me.

I didn't have to answer. Even if he didn't already know what that tour looked like, he saw it on my face.

He dropped his head back and looked up at the ceiling.

"So, if he can't force Ceecee out by neglecting the building, and he can't get her to pay more rent for the space because of the contract he had with her mom, he'll just sell and let the new owners end the bakery."

While the ceiling wasn't going to talk back to him, neither could I.

There weren't words in my vocabulary to help him at the moment.

Part of me wanted to know him better just so I could feel comfortable patting him on the arm and reassuring him.

But I didn't know him, and I couldn't bring myself to cross that line.

"I'm sure the new owners have to abide by the contract too," I said, my voice low because I wasn't sure. It made sense, but I had no idea. And even if I had the contract in front of me, I probably wouldn't be able to read through the legal jargon to see to the meaning.

He sat up and looked at me, nodding his head, but the small smile he gave me didn't show in his eyes.

"Maybe you're right."

I took another bite to avoid having to say anything else. He stood up, getting back to his task before he left me in the kitchen, looking around at all the equipment that had seen better days.

Ceecee's mom managed to draft a lease contract that kept her rent controlled and even transferred to her daughter. But did she think about what would happen if McCarthy sold the building?

Few people who owned the kind of money-making space McCarthy did ever sold in Seattle anymore. Even heirs of those who passed away just kept the properties and hired a rental agency to tend to them.

Why would someone sell a money maker?

Unless…

Now it was my turn to look up at the ceiling and wonder about the apartments above.

McCarthy didn't live in them. I wondered how leveraged he was. It could have been as simple as he was stuck and needed the money.

But Marcus gave me an idea.

I popped the rest of my snack in my mouth and downed the rest of my coffee. I needed to get the smaller part of the work done and figure some things out.

There was no way I was going to kill myself to do the big fix if it was going to benefit people who planned on putting Ceecee out of business.

If I could figure out everything I thought I needed to, I might save the day.

And, if I could do that, maybe I could keep Deacon, Katie, Olivia, and Campbell full of cinnamon rolls forever.

C E E C E E

arcus joined me behind the counter not long after Olivia left.

"We have a special order," I said, wiping things down and double checking how much we had left for the day in the cases.

"That's good," he muttered, not paying attention to me while he put the last tray of garlic rolls in the case.

"I don't think we'll have many more customers today. I might shut down early." I squinted out at the darkening sky. Rain still pelted down.

"Okay, no problem." He just stood there with his hands empty, staring down at the rolls.

Did he leave his brain in the kitchen?

"Maybe we should have a naked day tomorrow and work in only the aprons," I said.

"Hmm…"

"What is wrong with you right now?" I yelled and he jumped.

"I…" He looked around and stared back at me, his mouth open a fraction. "What?"

"You didn't listen to anything I was saying. Come on,

Marcus. What's going on?" I planted my hands on my hips and gave him the murder look. He was never this distracted. I didn't like it.

"Sorry, Cee." He ran his hands over his face and popped back out from them with a smile and his focus back. "For some reason, I was just lost in my head."

The door opened, and I had to let it go. But if he was even remotely not present again, I was going to find out what was making him act like he was drugged. Whether he wanted me to or not.

It was my turn to go on autopilot while we helped some customers. At least I was better at it than he was and at least he stayed engaged while they were there.

Eventually the trickle of constant people died down again.

Night had fully gripped the world through the windows. As the last of the customers opened the door to head out, the sound of the rain was even louder than it had been earlier.

"We are definitely shutting down early today," I said.

Marcus cut his eyes my way. But he pretended to keep his attention on the register and the breaking up of a roll of coins.

"Are you sure? You've been wanting to stay open lately."

He didn't say it in a negative way, just as an indifferent query. But still, it stung deep inside me.

It wasn't that I didn't want to stay open, but there was no way it wouldn't be cheaper to shut it down for the night than to spend the next three hours open hoping against common sense that someone would come in and buy the rest of the items in the cases.

"Ceecee," Theresa said from behind me, interrupting my internal waffling while I grimaced at my options.

"Oh, do you need anything?" I asked, turning to her with a smile.

She looked like she was startled and was trying not to show

it. With that expression on her face, the tool belt, the general no nonsense look of her, she seemed like someone who no one would want to mess with even though she was so small.

And it made my stomach flop over.

"No, I just wanted to show you that I'm done. Everything works again."

"Great." My voice squeaked and Marcus put a hand to his face, hiding what I just knew was an evil grin.

Theresa narrowed her eyes at both of us, but didn't say a word. Instead, she turned around and headed to the bathroom.

On my way past Marcus, I smacked his arm and he started shaking with silent laughter.

She stood to the side of the door, her bags of stuff in the hall behind her.

"I fixed the problem, and it should hold. But there is a bigger issue with the plumbing. Just keep an eye on it," she said.

The bathroom looked like it was back to normal, although there was a panel on the wall behind the toilet. But other than that, there was water in the bowl and none on the floor.

Leaning over, I hit the flush, and it worked.

"Seriously, thank you." I turned to look back at her and we paused, staring at each other for a moment too long.

But she broke the spell with a smile, a nod, and a wave of her hand to follow her to the kitchen.

Hustling after her, I couldn't get the grin off my face. Having things fixed felt like making the perfect recipe.

Well, if I didn't think about how much she was about to charge me.

Once we were in the kitchen and standing in front of the fridge, she paused and just looked at me, one corner of her mouth turning up.

I was about to ask her if I needed to buy a new one after all, but then I heard it.

The fridge was running.

"No way. You actually got it to cool." I grabbed the door handle to throw it open, but she put her hand on mine and made sure the door stayed shut.

Her hand on mine also shut down my brain. I opened and closed my mouth like a dying fish while I stared at her.

"Let it have time to get down to temperature again. It will take less time if you leave the door closed until it does. Then put the food back into it," she said, her voice softer and more intimate feeling than was necessary for the subject.

But it made my stomach flop again.

And when she pulled her hand back from mine, my fingers itched with the need to grab her hand back.

Instead, I shoved them into the apron and wrapped the fabric around them. Tight.

"Theresa, you saved me by doing this today."

"Don't worry about it. It's my job," she said, shaking her head and looking down at the ground.

"Right. I need to pay you then. How much did it end up being?" I asked, trying to reign in the ridiculous thumping of my heart. Clearly that was a lesson in futility. She didn't want me. She was just nice and she was just doing her job. I had to remember that.

"Here, I wrote it out for you," she said, handing me a small paper with the amount of labor and the amount of the items listed out on it.

I swallowed hard. It wasn't as bad as I was expecting. Not even close.

But having to shell out a few hundred dollars was still hard when that meant reexamining if I would still have enough to put a headstone on my mother's grave.

Wasting no time—mostly because I really didn't want to

think about it anymore than I already had to—I turned and headed to the front.

At least I was smart enough the night before to move the business checkbook and card to the register so I didn't have to worry about exposing the office.

Good job last night, me.

Theresa followed behind me, grabbing her bags as she went past them.

She came to the other side of the counter and leaned against it, all her bags dragging her down, while I filled out the check.

With the chime above the door jingling, the cold, wet air from outside swept in and sent the little paper invoice flying down to the floor at my feet.

"Ceecee," Mr. McCarthy said.

O *h, crap.*

Ceecee's face got three shades whiter as I watched her, my back to the door.

Marcus twisted his face into a rictus grin he probably thought looked happy to see the landlord.

I stayed facing forward, frozen and not able to think of a way out of this situation.

"Did you call someone in to work on something? Because if there is a problem, you should tell me."

His voice was laced with a fake sounding sympathy that made me want to lash out, to turn around and tell this guy off.

It no longer mattered if he was in dire need of money, or if he was just greedy. Fake caring was so gross.

One way or another, I was going to help Ceecee get out of this.

"Just on my way home from work and stopped in to see my girl," I said, waving a lazy hand over my shoulder while I glanced back before leaning across the counter toward Ceecee.

She paused with her hands on the checkbook and pen, her

eyes boring through my face like she was trying to figure out what was happening in my brain.

Good luck with that, because I wasn't really sure what I was doing either.

I tried to put all my persuasive abilities into my eyes and mouthed, '*Play along.*'

"Yep." She placed her hand on mine, tucking the pen and checkbook under my hands in the process. "But I can help you with something if you need it."

She looked back over my head at Mr. McCarthy by the door.

The man still had not moved. At least, I didn't hear any footsteps and she kept looking in the same spot.

How weird was this guy?

My excuse was brilliant. Anyone else would take care of their business quickly and leave people alone.

Apparently, this guy was not going to do that. I turned around and looked at him full on, crossing my arms over my chest and smiling like I was someone other than me. Someone tougher who was a little possessive.

Sure, I could play that part for a bit.

"Nice to see you're getting out there. I was worried about you after your mother passed." He nodded at Ceecee and walked further into the room, coming closer to me.

It took everything in me not to show how little I believed his concern for her on my face. Instead, I balled my hands into fists, hidden by my crossed arms.

"And, actually, could I get some of the garlic rolls? I'm having my…friends over for dinner tonight," he said.

Friends. Interesting way to describe the not exactly tourists from Scottsdale, who themselves said they were only here for business.

I stepped out of the way, leaning on the case by Marcus. He looked at me, eyes wide.

"Do I get an introduction? I'm McCarthy, and I own this building." He extended a hand for me to shake.

"Theresa," I said, grabbing his in an overly aggressive way. Most of the men that I worked with hated that.

He took a step back after I broke the contact, an odd array of expressions flitting across his face like he wasn't sure what to make of me.

"On your way home from work. So, what do you do? Clearly, it isn't baking," he said, laughing at his own joke.

"I'm a contractor," I said. There was no reason to lie about it now. Not as long as he bought my cover story.

Ceecee fumbled with a roll, dropping it back on the tray in the case.

"Well, maybe you can help me too." He brightened and turned away from Ceecee entirely, his focus narrowed in on me while his face settled into a look of real enjoyment.

"Maybe, what do you need help with?" It was an effort to keep the trepidation out of my voice, but he didn't seem to notice that the last thing I wanted to do was work for this guy.

"I've been in the market for a few fixer properties. Maybe you know of some I could look at?" He looked so excited. I tried to ignore the snarl forming on Ceecee's face and the horror in Marcus's eyes.

"You know there are a lot of people trying to get fixers right now."

He nodded and waved away my warning.

There weren't any I knew of off the top of my head except…

"Believe it or not, I do know of one. Are you wanting residential, commercial, or something like this that has both?"

Marcus scoffed and turned the noise into a coughing fit, excusing himself to the back when McCarthy looked his way with disgust.

Ceecee wilted and finished ringing up his purchase, putting the box on the counter.

"Preferably both, but almost anything. I've been looking around and I think there are some single-family homes that would convert well."

I nodded and pretended I didn't want to shake him and yell about the rising rents pricing people out of the city.

"In that case, I know of two properties. One is in Queen Anne and the other is in Fremont. Let me write down the addresses for you." I shot out a hand, making him jump back and out of the way although the grin and clear greed all over him didn't diminish at all.

Grabbing the pen from Ceecee and the box with his rolls in it, I jotted down two addresses.

"Thank you so much. This was a very good last-minute decision," McCarthy said, throwing a wad of bills on the counter that included at least three twenties. It must have been way more than his rolls cost. He snatched up the box and hustled out the front door.

Ceecee sighed behind me.

She was slumped against the counter, her head in her hands. Marcus popped out from around the corner.

"Whoever lives in those buildings, I feel bad for them," Marcus said and Ceecee nodded without lifting her head.

"No one lives in one of them. I know it because my mom was hired to tear it down and build a bigger building in its place for someone who will never sell it."

Marcus's jaw dropped open while Ceecee's head popped up.

And they both burst out laughing.

"You're kidding. That was an amazing performance. Thank you for covering for me," Ceecee said, straightening up and wiping the tears of laughter from the corner of her eyes.

"No problem." I fidgeted and grabbed my bags again.

She signed her check and handed it to me while Marcus kept laughing.

I smiled at them both and turned to go.

"Hey," Ceecee said, and I turned around again. "What's the other address?"

The grin on my face grew and I shoved the check into my pocket.

CEECEE

Theresa's smile seemed predatory, like she was a crocodile about to snap her mouth closed on a particularly stupid fish that swam into it.

"Sometimes we have very interesting clients," she said, turning halfway to the door. I thought she was going to leave it at that.

But she said, "Have you ever heard the rumors that some of the clubs in the area are owned by connected men?"

That was it. That was all she said, and she walked out the door.

"Ceecee, did she just say what I think she said?" Marcus asked next to me, all the laughter gone from his voice.

I nodded. Words failed me.

"So… she's for sure into girls," Marcus said, and I laughed.

"Yeah, well, no matter how into girls she is, I don't know if I will ever see her again. I'm not sure that helps me. Her work is done here." I wandered along the cases, checking to see how much we still had left in them.

"But you're friends with her friends. You could see her again if you wanted to." He leaned against the counter and tilted his chin up, staring down his nose at me like he had made some masterful point.

I rolled my eyes and made a mental note to give it one more hour before I closed the doors.

"Manufacturing a way to see her again by pseudo stalking our mutual acquaintances doesn't scream romantic to me, you weirdo," I said, raising a brow at him.

"Weirdo is a title I wear with pride. No one, even the tragically normal, wants to be called a normie so you need to do better than that." He turned on a heel and started to walk down the hall.

"Hey, where are you going?" I called after him.

"To load up the fridge again and see if I can get some of these coolers cleaned out."

Good point. There was still a lot I needed to do, even if I did shut things down early.

Only two more people came in the next hour, so I called it quits on the day.

Locking the front door, I heard Marcus yell from the kitchen. I dropped the key on the floor and ran.

Grabbing the door jamb to the kitchen so I swung around it and sent myself careening into Marcus as he ran out.

"What's going on?" I screamed.

At the same time, he yelled, "The oven."

Over his shoulder, one of the ovens hung open, heat waves poured out of it, and a thin tendril of smoke wafted up from toward the ceiling.

"Not now," I said, my voice as thin and insubstantial as the smoke.

"I didn't do anything. I turned it on to preheat so I could make us something to celebrate with, and when I opened it to put it in, there was a snap and the smoke," he stammered.

Only then did I notice the small batch of cinnamon rolls spilled on the door to the oven and dripping down the side to the floor.

"Are there enough ovens to keep working?" he asked.

"Yeah — Yes." I nodded, because yes, there were, and I was going to make it work.

But the truth was, the kitchen already wasn't as well-appointed as any of my competition and didn't have nearly the same capacity.

One less oven would mean even more baking during the day because there was no way I would have enough time to make it all beforehand.

And it made even the thought of taking on more custom orders like Olivia's seem like a terrible idea.

"I need to fix it soon, though," I said, going closer to the oven, turning it off, and assessing how much of a mess I needed to clean up.

"Good thing we know a capable fixing girl," Marcus almost yelled in relief.

For some reason he seemed happy, but even if Theresa could fix it, I didn't have the money to pay for it at the moment.

Marcus didn't know that.

I had to remind myself that I kept most of my worries about money from him. Because if things got much worse, I was going to have to let him go and try to do everything myself.

But I nodded and gestured to him to go close up.

Even though I loved him, I needed to be alone.

Alone with my broken mess.

I should get used to it.

Adjusting the ice pack on my knee meant re-situating my wet hair as I leaned back in my chair.

My room was in a sad state, and I should have cleaned it. But I had zero...no, less than zero interest in doing that at the moment.

In fact, I wasn't doing anything but getting stuck in my own head.

The whole time I was in the bath, the entire time I was changing into my pajamas and limping around my room, I was actually in the little bakery on Pike.

Downstairs, my mom was going to call me any minute to come get the takeout she ordered for dinner.

But up here, in the same room I grew up in and only left for a little while for college, I wasn't poring over paperwork for the business or schedules for the crews.

Nope, I was trying to think of a way to save Ceecee.

I reached for my phone and hesitated before texting Olivia.

You know I blame you for this.

My phone dinged with a text faster than I expected. She was usually working.

So you like her?

How did I answer that?

Of course, I liked her. But more than that, her landlord reminded me of my mom, and I wanted to help her stick it to him in a way that made me question how far I had actually come with my mom.

Did you know she is having trouble with her space?

There was little chance Olivia knew that, but I had to check.

What trouble?

Part of me didn't think Ceecee would be happy with me talking about this, but I needed to talk to someone and Olivia was good people.

Her landlord wants to up rents.

Olivia responded so fast I wondered that she had time to type it out.

No. I promise I didn't. But it shouldn't surprise me. Lots of people are getting priced out right now. I'm having a hard time finding a space too.

Since when was Olivia looking for a space?

??? Is Joe's moving?!

Maybe I could have put down my phone and ignored the conversation with her before, but now I stared at the screen, afraid to blink.

Joe's couldn't move.

That building was like home.

I knew I could go there with the cheerleading squad, or by myself when my own home had been the toughest, during the time Olivia and I dated and just after it. Joe's was happy and positive.

Sure, it would probably be the same atmosphere even if the

building was different, but there was something to be said for the familiar alcoves and the unique quirks of the place.

Of course not. My parents own the building.

I knew that and it still gave me a chance to take a deep breath.

But Campbell and I would like to live together, and I thought finding an apartment above a space he could use as a pool hall would be perfect.

Campbell and Olivia wanted to move in together.

Well, well, look at you. On the hunt for a love nest. If I find anything through Mom, I'll let you know.

I leaned my head back, and looked up at the ceiling, not bothering to drop the genuine smile from my face.

Even if I had been surrounded, I still would have smiled at the good news of Olivia and Campbell doing so well.

She deserved the best. And even I couldn't argue that he was the best for her.

One day, I hoped I would find a relationship like theirs.

My phone dinged in my hand again.

That would be so great. Thanks T!

No one else called me T except Olivia, and it had been a long time since she did. I was glad it was back.

Of course

"Theresa, dinner," Mom called from downstairs, and I had to set my phone aside to strap my brace back on my knee.

Getting back to my feet made all the aches in my leg return.

Making my way down the stairs was a special kind of torture, but Mom would never agree to bring me my dinner. Not when she saw me avoiding the stairs as a weakness.

"If I ever find a cheap space for the bakery, or one for Olivia, it will have an elevator," I mumbled to myself.

But it brought me up short at the bottom of the stairs.

A space that would accommodate a bakery, a pool hall, and some apartments…

Did such a place exist?

I picked up the pace heading into the kitchen.

Mom was putting her dinner on a plate, a glass of wine in her other hand. She glanced up at me, her smile tight.

"Your dinner is in the bag," she said and grabbed her plate, turning to walk away.

"Wait," I said, getting to the island and leaning on it without letting her know I was favoring my leg.

She turned back to me with her eyebrows high and the look on her face said I had a limited number of minutes to keep her attention.

"How hard would it be to find a property—even if it needed work—that could house two small businesses and at least two apartments?"

If I had thrown her a bomb, I don't think it would have made quite the impact my question did.

Mom was never stumped. But she looked as if I just asked her to tell me about the math behind chaos theory.

"Are you planning on starting a business?" she finally asked, a smile blooming on her face.

Honesty was probably the best bet, but if I told her the truth, would she be as helpful?

I doubted it.

"Yes. I have an idea. And I know someone who has the experience needed to make it a success who would be willing to come on board. But I need to figure out if it's even feasible first." In my head I crossed my fingers that she wouldn't ask for specifics.

"Grab your dinner and come in the dining room with me," she said, her grin wide as she turned to head that way.

Okay, first step was done.

Now, all I had to do was sell her on the idea of a pool hall with a shark as a partner and the world's best cinnamon roll bakery next door.

Sure, because those things went together.

I sighed and followed after her, crossing my fingers that being this honest with her wouldn't be a complete disaster.

My back was killing me.

Days of sleeping on my mattress on the floor in the office left me with aches in places I was unaware there were things to ache. I couldn't fit my box spring in the space I wedged the mattress into so I had no choice, but it sucked.

Somehow, I needed to rearrange the office so that my mattress wasn't crammed between the filing cabinets and the wall. Maybe if it was able to lay all the way flat it wouldn't hurt me so badly.

I stared at the stupid thing for a few minutes more before I closed up the room and headed into the kitchen.

Today I was going to get a call back from the power company. Since I was spending all my time here, the last little while was going to be more expensive, and I wanted to know how much more expensive the next bill would be since we just ended a period yesterday. I hoped they would try and estimate for me what the one after that would cost with the increased average too, but I wasn't sure they would give me that.

"Please let moving into the office pay off," I said, closing my eyes and hoping the universe heard me.

My personal bank account was also supposed to take a massive hit today when I paid for Mom's headstone. I needed to do it. The ache in my back was nothing compared to the guilt that washed over me every time I thought about how bad of a daughter I was for not doing it.

The back door opened as I pulled the first batch of dough out to get started on the actual baking.

"Hey," Marcus called from the hallway.

"In here," I yelled back. There was no sense in letting him walk unawares into the office and making him go through this with me any more than he already was.

"Did you decide what you're going to do for Olivia's order tomorrow?" he asked, coming into the kitchen and tying his apron on.

"Not yet. It's hard because I want something that's a little more than just the usual and I don't know Dominican flavors the way I should." I grabbed another batch of dough. The movements of the process in the morning were so automatic that I didn't have to think about them.

"Dominican flavors?" He grabbed his own supplies and set up at the other station to start on other things.

"Yes. Carmen, the birthday girl, is from the Dominican Republic, and I thought it would be nice if at least some of the flavors were something that would bring the tropical, the island, to her here."

I had two whole batches of dough rolled out. They took up the entirety of my workspace when I started to turn them into Mom's famous cinnamon rolls.

"Oh, I like that idea. So, you're trying to find a flavor or two that would brighten up her birthday in the grayness of the weather." He smiled and set the ovens with practiced movements that I appreciated.

"Exactly. Food is more than just calories to put in your body." He nodded along as I said it. I grinned.

"You always say that. And you know what I always say?" His smile took on a wicked tilt that made me stop and brace myself for whatever he was going to say next.

"What do you always say?" May as well ask him since he clearly wanted me to, and get it out of the way so I could get back to work.

"That you should call Theresa." He cocked his head at me and raised his brows high.

"Stop, Marcus. That ship has sailed. I told you, I don't think I'll see her again." I finished what I was doing and cut the dough into strips.

"Ugh. Every party has a pooper. That's why we invited you." He stuck his tongue out at me and went back to his work too.

"Now *that*, is what you always say." I shook my head and laughed at him.

"Come on, Cee. You need to get out. You need to see her again. You know I'm right. You can't spend every minute of the day here."

He may not have known I was living in the office, but his words did make me swallow hard. I felt bad that it was worse than he even knew.

"Marcus?" I asked, starting to roll the dough up.

"Yeah?" He turned to me, his face open and unassuming.

"When was the last time you went on a date?" I asked and his mouth dropped open.

"Dirty tricks, you." He turned his back to his work and I laughed.

"Have you tested any ideas for Carmen's recipe?" he asked

sometime later when we were loading the trays in the front of the store while still more baked in the kitchen.

"I tried two last night in single batches, but they didn't work out. I'm going to try some more tonight, I think. What I need is some taste testers," I said.

"Taste testers?" He looked around himself and back at me. "I'm right here, Ceecee."

Laughing, I bumped into his shoulder and made my way past him to take another tray out of the oven.

"Yeah, but I need someone who doesn't automatically love everything I make," I yelled back at him.

"Telling you all your recipes are good isn't a lie if it's true." His voice was so strong it bounced off the clean metal surfaces of the kitchen, giving it a strange reverberating quality as if it was the voice of some food god.

"Just because you're loud doesn't make you right."

Even his laughter made its way to me.

But my good humor died while looking around at the kitchen. It was getting harder by the day to keep up with the amount of baking we had to do while one of the ovens was down and we both needed to be at the front so often.

How was I going to make it work when the weekend and good weather came at the same time, and we were slammed?

It turned out that I didn't need to wait for that weekend to find myself in the weeds.

That day, for the first time in a while, the rain clouds broke by nine in the morning.

We were so inundated with customers that Marcus was stuck in the front and I was stuck in the kitchen until two in the afternoon.

By then I needed to order more ingredients, I had my third batch of dough getting ready, and I was dialing Olivia because I didn't have Theresa's number.

"Mom, please. Can you get Wade, Tony, someone else to do it? I need to do this." I was so close to getting on my knees and begging, or stepping into her face and screaming. I had to hold a hand against my stomach to keep me back.

"This is your job, Theresa. I can't give you a bunch of special time off because you're my daughter. That's not how business works." She shook her head and went back to her report.

Business...

"I understand that, and I wouldn't ask except this is part of what I need to do for that business idea I have. There's no point in looking for the property if I can't get the business ready for when we have property, right?" Okay, so I lied. But there it was my best chance to get her to let me off the schedule.

She narrowed her eyes at me, not tilting her head up, just squinting her eyes as she looked at me through her lashes.

Breathe, I reminded myself.

Mom was like a shark. She could smell blood in the water.

The only thing saving me from her sniffing out every single

thing I did that that she wouldn't approve of, was long practice. And that wasn't foolproof.

"Fine. But don't make a habit of this, Theresa. Until you aren't working for me, you need to actually work for me." She went back to her report, and I was dismissed.

I didn't hustle away because doing so would've tipped her off.

Some stupid, naive part of me couldn't wait to get to the bakery.

Part of me had hope that it wasn't just my work that Ceecee wanted.

Taking my phone out of my pocket, I texted Olivia.

Tell Ceecee I'm on my way

A second later it chimed back at me.

How did you get your mom to let you out of work?

Olivia remembered. When we were together it was one of the things that drove her bananas. How my mom's capital type A and beliefs meant I was capital type A by coercion.

Anything for business.

If she only knew how much my mom was doing to help me get my 'business' idea off the ground—the one I made up on the spot and had no intention of actually doing—she would have been shocked.

My phone chimed again.

I have no idea what that means, but I told Ceecee you're going to help. And, hey. I think you should not charge her for this one. Let me pick up the tab.

Outside the house, with my hand on my truck door, I stopped and read the message more than once before I could form a response.

What are you talking about?

It didn't take long for her to text me back, which was good

because putting all my weight on my good leg and not moving was starting to be painful.

She's good people and if she has to move her business, I'm not sure she has the funds for that. Let me help.

Chewing on my lip, I thought about it.

Olivia was doing well. Joe's was busier than ever, and she used the increase in business to pay off all the restaurant's debts. She had been working since she was too young to actually do it and she never spent money on anything.

Meanwhile, I was trying to save up enough to do what I actually wanted to, which was buy a building and fix it up so Campbell could have his pool hall, and Ceecee could have her bakery.

And Ceecee...Ceecee deserved better than her landlord and better than scraping by.

Okay. But thank you, Olivia. I mean it. Love you.

She would know what I meant.

Love you too. And I'm glad you're helping her.

I couldn't stop the grin that popped onto my face as I climbed into my truck.

Olivia was right. Ceecee was good people. And I was glad I was helping her, too.

Especially since it meant I could see her again.

Although, I did wonder if her landlord would show up again, and what he would think about the little mistake I made with the addresses.

My smile only grew as I headed to The Bake Place.

"She's on her way," I said, putting down my phone, biting my lip, and wondering if I made the right decision or not.

"When will she get here?" Marcus asked, not doing a good job of keeping the smirk off his face.

"I'm not sure," I said, throwing a wadded-up napkin at him, "But I am sure that you need to be out front today. Because depending on how long it takes her back here, I could be doing the constant baking thing again."

He dropped his head back and looked at the ceiling, his shoulders slumping.

"Between yesterday and today, I am going to be too tired to do anything after work."

"Sorry." And I was. I hated making him feel like working here was a burden.

Marcus straightened up and smiled at me.

"Don't worry, Cee. You already pay me enough." He laughed and went out front.

The pay thing was an ongoing discussion. He complained

that I paid him too much, but he didn't do it too loudly. He knew as well as I did that it was next level expensive to live in the city, and I barely paid him enough to be able to do it. That, and we both knew I needed him and I would pay him more if I could.

It didn't matter how much I needed him though. If something didn't give, if I couldn't find another way to bring in some more funds, I was going to have to let him go. His salary was my last available expenditure to cut.

Even thinking about it that way, as an expenditure, made my heart ache.

Marcus deserved better than working here for the rest of his life.

He only stayed to help, and every day it looked more and more likely that I was going to have to force his hand to find something that could be better for him.

But that was letting myself off the hook for hurting him.

Ugh. I punched the dough in my hands. I had over-kneaded it to the point of turning it into sticky glop.

"Hey, can you put on some music?" I yelled to Marcus, who whooped in response.

A stream of wild dance music floated out of the speakers a moment later.

"Very funny!" I shook my head and finished cleaning up my bad dough mess.

The music cut off and between it and the next, his laughter was louder than the speakers had been.

Not long after, the sounds of fun, upbeat oldies started. It was so much better for our mix of customers. And it was what I needed. I took a deep breath and let it take my mind away.

By the time I was in a groove, the doors were open, Marcus was running around like a headless chicken helping everyone out front, and I was singing along to Lollipop.

Tingles spread down my arms. It felt like I was being watched.

Assuming that Marcus was coming in for something, I spun around thinking I could just grab it for him. Seeing Theresa standing in the doorway, I froze. Her tool belt was low on her hips, loaded down with all manner of things I didn't understand, and she had two bags slung over her shoulders again.

"Hi," she said, a smile forming on her face.

I pawed my hair out of my eyes with the back of my hand and offered a shaky smile back while I tried to figure out how long she had been standing there.

Finally, I decided to ask.

"How long have you been here?" My voice was quavery and didn't match the tune of the song still playing in the background.

"Long enough to know that you should come to karaoke with us sometime. I suck, but it's fun." Her smile didn't falter even when she insulted her singing ability, but it made me nervous.

Was that a friendly invitation? Offhand comment? Or… something that made sense out of the feeling of champagne bubbles in my stomach?

"So, direct me to what needs to be fixed." She waved a hand and I realized I was still for too long.

"Oh, um, see, I need to ask you something first."

Her only response was to raise a brow at me in waiting.

"Can you give me an estimate before you start on the work, because if it's too much I might need to have a little time to figure out how to pay for it." Damn, that was rough. It was hard to even look at her while I fell all over my own words.

"Don't worry about it, Ceecee. I don't like your landlord. Let's just get you fixed up to find a way around him, huh?" She walked toward me. The limp from her knee brace was more apparent when she was weighed down with all that stuff.

I bit my lip, trying to figure out if I should take this gift that she was giving me out of spite for him, or if I should turn her down. Because this was a lot for her to do for me. We barely knew each other, really. Would she do so much just because we both knew Olivia?

She reached out a tentative hand and wiped a tear off my cheek that I wasn't even aware had fallen. Her touch was light and soft even though her fingers were rough and calloused.

"Please don't cry," she said.

That was it. She didn't tell me not to, tell me I didn't have a reason, or even try and say she understood. She just asked me.

I nodded and wiped my cheeks myself, blinking until I got control over my face again and smiled.

"Thank you," I said.

She gave me a soft smile and tiny bow of her head.

"Okay, so this oven was heating up the other day, there was a pop, and some smoke came out. I don't know what all you'll have to do to fix it," I said, leading her to the stupid old thing that decided to betray me.

"No worries. You go back to singing and I'll get to work." She set down her bags and started checking it all out.

I watched for a minute before I washed my hands and went back to what I was doing.

Eventually, she pulled the big thing out from the wall in a move that made my arms sore just watching her do it. But she didn't seem fazed by it at all.

The only thing she had trouble with was getting up and down from the floor with her knee the way it was. Which reminded me, I didn't actually know.

"Hey, I hope this isn't a crappy, intrusive question," I said, but I knew it was, so I looked down at the dough I was working while I asked, "But, what happened to your knee? And how long will it be like that?"

"Ah, well, it is intrusive, but everyone wants to know, so..." She set down the tool she was using that I couldn't even name—although I had grown much more familiar with them in recent years.

"I was a cheerleader, on scholarship, blew out my knee. It happens." She waved a hand in the air.

But it was there, in her eyes, that it was a lot more than something that just happened. At least it was to her.

"Anyway, I came home, had surgery, more than once, work for my mom because I didn't know what else to do, and hopefully in a few months my knee will be close to what it was before. Now, I'm here. Fixing the oven." She smiled, but it was hollow before she went back to what she was doing.

For some reason, even after the issues I had with cheerleaders in high school, and even after thinking the worst of her for suspecting she was one, her story made me like her more.

"That sucks. I'm sorry. I don't know what I would do if I lost this place. It's the only thing I've ever planned on, the only thing I want to do," I said and shrugged, hoping she understood what I meant. That I understood what she had lost was important to her.

She sat on the floor and looked up at me for a while, her eyes softening and making her even more beautiful.

I went back to work. If I stared at her much longer, I would be telling on myself. She was the only thing helping to keep the business going in a lot of ways. No matter how much I wanted her to touch my face again, I couldn't risk it.

*M*oments before, Ceecee's movements were graceful and fluid with an economy of motion that showed just how at home she was in the kitchen. When she noticed me, they turned awkward and staccato.

She had to pick up and put things down twice before she grabbed the thing she meant to and started to get back into the flow of her work.

Maybe I was wrong, but I thought she was flustered. I thought *I* got her flustered.

I smiled and went back to work myself.

Hopefully, that meant I would manage to get her to come with me some time.

Even if it wasn't karaoke, I wanted to see her again. I wanted to touch her again.

The screwdriver in my hand was suspended in air, not doing me any good.

Come on, Theresa. Get it together.

I went back to putting all my tools away so they weren't

scattered across the floor, and shoved myself back up to standing.

Once I was upright, I put the heating element in the little bag I brought and slung it over my arm.

In the process, I realized she was doing something different than the kinds of things I saw in her case before.

"What are those?" I asked, stepping closer to her workstation, and pointing at the tray of small flower-shaped cups. No baking dish I had ever seen looked like them.

"Those will be cupcakes for Carmen's birthday party. I still need to figure out a special recipe to do for some of the order. I'm thinking something that has flavors of summer, or something tropical. But what I'm trying right now is chocolate cupcake with boiled meringue icing." She finished pouring the mixture into the little cups and I was stuck there staring at the cupcakes.

"You don't do these regularly, do you?" I had to ask. Maybe I just wasn't here for when she did it.

"No," she said with a laugh, stepping back and double-checking something about the pour she had just finished. "There are specialty stores in Seattle for that already, so I just focus on all the other baked goods."

But cupcakes would be really popular, especially unique ones like the one she was making that made my mouth water.

"I think you would sell those all day. I mean...I would buy them," I said.

"You haven't even tasted them." She smiled and rolled her eyes at me as she popped them into one of the working ovens.

"Right, but I've tasted your other treats. Loved those. And chocolate with meringue? Yes, please. Just think about doing some cupcakes. I think they would be a big hit." I walked past her. I really did need to get to my appliance parts guy, because he was my best bet outside of ordering it. And none of us wanted me to wait around for an order.

The front of the bakery was a mad house. Marcus was fast, but there were just too many people shoved in there together for him to be able to keep up.

Okay, new plan.

Get the part, grab a change of clothes, haul it back here, fix the oven, and then help Marcus.

How hard could it be to do the work in the front?

Sure, I had never dealt with anyone in a retail capacity, but it couldn't be that bad.

But making my way through the crowd was like negotiating with a nest of vipers, even though I was obviously not heading in the direction of the counter and wouldn't be cutting in front of anyone waiting in line.

People sneered and complained and bumped into me.

What was wrong with everyone?

Getting outside was a relief. And it was more than just the fresh air after wading through so many people's different colognes.

On the way back to the truck, I had to watch my steps on the cobblestones. At least this morning I was here early. It wasn't nearly the hike from the other day.

Once I was in the truck, I ticked off every single person looking for a parking space by getting out my phone and texting Olivia even though she probably wouldn't get it until way after I was done for the day.

How do you and Campbell handle dealing with the customers? The bakery customers are all being pushy.

I always assumed it would be easy. Olivia had social anxiety, and she did it all the time.

Maybe I was just a jerk.

Turning into the delivery spot for the parts guy, the thought of me being especially bad with people wouldn't leave my brain.

By the time I opened the door to the overcrowded shop, I was grinding my teeth.

"Who peed in your oatmeal?" Gaylen said. He was placing items on a shelf that looked like it was about to shatter under the weight.

"Very funny. I was just thinking." My face split into a grin the second I looked at him, no matter what it was doing before.

He had that effect.

And it didn't hurt that Old Blue Eyes was playing over the speaker system.

Gaylen always had the best music.

"In that case, this is now a no thinking zone, my dear," he said, smiling and heading over to me.

He put a hand on my shoulder and all the stress of the last week fell away.

No matter how old Gaylen got, he was still spry and smiling, always here when I just wanted to hide away.

There was even a recliner in the back, surrounded by all manner of parts that smelled vaguely of metal and a dizzying array of fluids like oil and something sweet I assumed was from the perpetually half-broken air conditioner.

All through high school I spent at least an hour a week in that recliner doing homework, just to get a break.

"So, do you need the chair?" he asked, stepping back and letting go of my shoulder.

"Not today, but I might when I'm done with this job." I laughed and he nodded.

"Okay, so what are we looking for?" He was already scanning the shelves. His system for storing things was known only to him.

"This," I said, pulling the heating element out of the bag.

He whistled and adjusted his glasses to look at the plug-in a little closer.

"Come on, I'm not sure if it's still here, but I know I had one at some point." He walked three rows of shelves over and lead me a little more than halfway along the shelf.

Sure enough, there was a massive pile of heating elements wedged between three carburetors on one side and a stack of ice cube trays on the other.

"Ice cube trays?" I asked, picking one up.

"Believe it or not, those are hard to keep in stock. A lot of people don't have ice makers, but not a lot of stores sell them like they used to." He dug through the pile of elements, comparing a few to the one I held up for him and discarding each.

Finally, he sighed and looked at me with a frown.

"Sorry, kid. I can get it here by next Monday, though." He patted my shoulder as he walked past me, not bothering to wait for me to tell him to go ahead and order it.

He would order it. He probably knew the exact part number. And he for sure knew what kind of appliance it came from.

I put the stupid broken element back in my bag and rubbed a hand over my face.

This was exactly what I didn't want to happen.

Ceecee might be upset.

Because I sure was.

I brought out another tray to Marcus and put it in the case.

We only had one customer at the moment, which was good because I didn't want to talk to anyone.

All I wanted to do was check the clock and get back to work.

"Ceecee, don't look at the clock again. She will be here when she gets here," Marcus said, passing by me with two boxes to take payment for them.

He was right, but he was also too late.

I saw the time. But it didn't matter. There was too much to do and not enough minutes to do it in regardless of whether Theresa came back.

Rushing back to the kitchen, my feet aching, I gave myself one second to close my eyes, breathe, feel sorry for myself, and allow the pain of too busy a day to wash through me.

Then I shoved it all away again and focused on what I needed to do.

A long time ago, Mom taught me how to give myself a space small enough that it wouldn't take over my ability to keep going, but large enough that it wasn't gnawing at me as much.

Eventually, I was going to have to find a time to get to the laundromat, too.

It was an errant thought, but it made continuing to work much harder, undoing the effects of Mom's trick.

After another twenty minutes of constant movement, I had the block of time I needed to be able to finish the cupcakes.

Everything was cool now. I was out of time to mess with the flavors anymore, so chocolate with boiled meringue was going to be the special kind along with Key Lime. It wasn't a new flavor for me, but it was light and bright like I wanted.

I still wound up with four extras because I needed a taste test. And if I didn't make one for Marcus he would kill me.

Making the meringue had a rhythm to it. It was different than kneading the dough or even decorating the tops, but they were all part of the same dance class. The kind of class taught by the grownups of the family to the kids.

I felt my mom every time I fell into those kinds of movements, found the steady beat at the heart of the kitchen, and allowed it to dictate how I made my way through something.

Even when I changed the ingredients, I followed the steps she taught me when I was small.

A long time ago, she used to have a song. It wasn't singing so much as it was a low, thrumming harmony that she accompanied some of our moments in the kitchen with.

The words didn't matter. She changed them all the time.

But I hummed the tune to myself as I finished the test batch for Olivia's order.

Something made with Mom's song in it always turned out better than something missing that soul.

And I wanted these to be good.

From the front, a peal of wild laughter reminded me I

couldn't afford to take any more time with the cupcakes. They were done for now.

I set them aside and started back into the too hurried, and too utilitarian portion of my work.

On the days I had time to prep everything properly, got almost all the baking done in the morning, and had plenty of time in the kitchen to work on special things while Marcus ran the front, there was nowhere else I wanted to be.

But on days like today—and all the ones staring back at me from the future—I wondered what it would feel like to bake in someone else's kitchen.

I wondered what it would be like to be able to just bake and let other people worry about the paperwork, the orders, dealing with customers, cleaning, worrying about the money, and all the planning.

Nice work if you can get it.

Even while I thought about it, though, part of me would be crumbs forever if I lost Mom's bakery.

The actual, visualized, thought of working in someone else's kitchen, following someone else's recipe, made my stomach want to rebel.

No. I needed The Bake Place and it needed me.

Mom was gone and the only thing I had left were memories and flavors.

"Okay, focus," I muttered out loud.

"Having trouble focusing?" Theresa said from the doorway, her hands in her pockets, her tool belt gone, and no bags hanging off of her. Maybe it was being physically lighter that made her face seem more open.

"Yes. Too much happening, but don't worry about that. What's the word?"

Please don't ask me more about what I was thinking, I begged her in my mind.

Not only was I unsure whether I was capable of explaining it, I wasn't sure she would want to hear me yammer on. Part of me wondered if I wasn't so far in my head because of her.

"Okay." She moved further into the room, taking a deep breath and making me bite my lip and cringe. "Do you want good or bad?"

"That bad?" I asked, my voice coming out whinier than I wanted it to be, but her small smile was sympathetic.

"Gaylen doesn't have the part, and if he doesn't, no one does. But he did know the part and was able to order it. It will be here in about a week."

"Crap." I looked around the kitchen, but even this familiar place felt overwhelming at the moment. "That's okay. I suspected it would happen."

I had to find a way to pay the overtime I needed to for Marcus to work every day of that with me.

THERESA

{P}oor Ceecee looked so different than she had when I walked in. I wanted to take it all back and tell her I would find the part.

But there was no way someone else would have one for a stove so old. Only Gaylen collected parts that way.

Well…Gaylen was the only one I knew, and therefore the only packrat parts guy that mattered. Anyone else would have to order it for me, too. And none of them would come find me when they got the part because they knew it was important.

"I'm sorry. I really am."

She nodded, taking in a big breath, standing up straighter, and fixing a smile to her face like she was gluing it there.

"Um," I looked around and tried to think of some reason I should stay, and help in the front. But the look on her face told me I let her down. It was more than a delay, this was a huge problem.

The clothes on my back, the ones I changed into to stay and help, suddenly made me itch. There was no way my presence was going to be a good thing. Not right now.

"I'll be back as soon as the part comes in," I said, knowing it wasn't enough and too afraid to do more.

There was nothing else I could think to do.

With all my stuff already in the truck, I couldn't even delay by picking up tools. I turned to leave.

"Theresa," she said, and I looked back at her over my shoulder. "Thank you. I don't know what I would have done if you weren't able to fix all that you have already. So, thanks."

I nodded and left the kitchen. The smell of fresh bread and the sweet tang of the cupcakes she was making followed me out to the door.

Normally, I would have bought something to take home with me, but even the scent of the bakery made me want to run as far and as fast as I could. The last thing I needed at the moment was to drag it all home with me.

Plus, I had no idea how to stand there and make small talk with Marcus after I failed.

Failure was too familiar.

We had become a team. One where I kept doing all the work, and it kept winning.

The worst group project ever.

At the truck with all my bags piled next to me, the thought of going home made me want to scream.

But the best thing about friends owning a restaurant was that you didn't have to call ahead if you wanted to see them.

I grabbed my phone anyway and shot a text to everyone else, letting them know I was going to hole up at Joe's if they wanted to join me.

Hopefully Katie and I could have a conversation and patch up whatever had gone wrong last time I saw her.

And then I shoved all hope away as I drove through the streets of Seattle, sending sprays of water up from the rain-soaked pavement.

Lately my track record sucked, and I didn't want to risk jinxing it.

Other people's hope was like a shield for them from the negative things in the world. Mine was like an invitation for those negative things to target me.

Hope and I were no longer friends.

By the time I got to Joe's and parked the truck, my knee was starting to seize up.

I limped my way through the parking lot to the employee's entrance. Technically, I wasn't supposed to use it. But Olivia gave me permission when I was still on crutches, so I didn't have to go all the way around to the front door.

The kitchen of Joe's was warm and, although it was bustling, there was a relaxed air to everyone in it.

My shoulders slumped. The tension in my neck released from just being here.

But the limp only got worse.

It was like the closer I got to sitting in one of the alcoves, to being off my feet, the more my legs wanted to give out and be done for the day.

Campbell almost bumped into me with a tray loaded down with plates as he made his way into the kitchen.

"Hey, Theresa. I'll be out in a second. Just sit where you want." He kept moving, gracefully avoiding a collision with me as I attempted to pivot in my brace.

"Thanks," I said, hoping he knew I meant more than just the table.

Once upon a time I was just as graceful, even if he could still beat me in a game of pool no matter how hard he tried to teach me and no matter how long I kept trying to learn.

Along the wall closest to the kitchen was our table, the one I thought of as ours.

My friends and I usually sat nearest to where Olivia and Campbell were working so we could distract them as much as possible.

Part of me just wanted to drop into one of the chairs I passed—even though the alcove was close, and I really wanted the enclosed safety of it.

I finally got to the alcove and collapsed into the cushioned booth, leaning against the back of the seat and closing my eyes.

The sounds of the restaurant around me amplified at first, but soon they fell back to an undulating hum I couldn't pick single noises out of.

The volume changing buzz and the scent of pizza mixed with some of the newer menu items Olivia and Campbell added, made my stomach growl and my brain tingle with all the best memories. Which somehow made it all worse.

"You okay?" Olivia asked, her voice low and soft, but still managing to break through the fog I was falling into.

I opened my eyes, and she was sitting across from me, sliding a soda toward me and taking a sip of hers.

"Did I take you away from something? You can go take care of your stuff." I took a sip of my cold drink, looking down at the table.

"That wasn't an answer," she said, her mouth pressed in a thin line.

Maybe it wasn't such a great idea to come here. Olivia knew me too well.

"Honest?" She nodded and I sighed, dropping my head back to stare at the curved ceiling of the alcove above my head. "I can't even say I'm okay, because I'm in a mood. But there's nothing really wrong. Does that make sense?"

Sneaking a glance at her, she gave a grim smile, and took a sip of her drink.

"Yeah. I'm with you, actually."

"Wait," I popped my head up and looked at her full on. The usual Olivia—the one deliriously happy since Campbell came along and her mom was declared cancer free—was gone. This Olivia looked like she was about to snap at someone. "What's going on?"

She sighed and rolled her head around on her neck.

"Here's the thing: Nothing is going on. It sounds stupid, and like I'm complaining when I have this great life. But I have plans, you know? Things I want to do. Things I need to make happen. And are any of those plans working for me at the moment? Big nope."

I nodded.

Complaining about something wrong wasn't really accurate for me. It just wasn't exactly right. And Olivia was in the same boat in some way.

"Brought you the usual," Campbell said, putting a plate of Carmen Yucca Fries and the fruit dessert pizza I was currently obsessed with on the table. He paused with his arms outstretched and his hand still under the tray.

"Are..." he started and swallowed, "You both look pissed off."

"No," I said, shaking my head. Although I couldn't quite make my mouth smile, which showed how not entirely true that statement was.

"We're not really furious at anything, it's just a..." Olivia waved a hand in the air and looked to me for the rest of her sentence.

"Communal madness," I said, and it seemed right.

She nodded and Campbell raised his eyebrows, looking back and forth between us like he still didn't really understand.

I didn't expect him to, but there wasn't anything else I could say to further explain this weird state Olivia and I shared for the moment.

At least if I was going to be in this place in my head, I had someone else there with me— over different things, sure, but still. Olivia feeling the same way, even a little bit, at least made me feel less crazy.

"That's all the coolers taken care of," Marcus said, walking in the back door and shaking the rain off his coat before he hung it up on the day of the party.

"Good. Thank you. Are you going to come with me for the delivery?" I asked, looking at the things left to sell that would just have to be put on clearance tomorrow if we both left the bakery at the same time during our normal hours.

"Are you sure you want me to do that? Shouldn't I stay here?" he asked, putting his apron back on and wiping the rain from his shoes one more time.

I looked out the window at the downpour and the orange cones the construction crews put up to show people the narrow path they could use to get to the front door. It was right around where they now had cobblestones pulled out of the street and piled up to be put back later.

"Chances are small that we'll get much in the way of customers today anyway." And there wasn't a damn thing I could do about the road work. Of all the times the area had been surrounded by construction over the years, this was for sure the worst.

"You're not wrong. And it's a wet mess out there on top of it." Marcus rubbed his hands up and down his arms like the chill had made its way into his bones and he was struggling to warm up.

"Mom used to talk about how after the earthquake in 2001—I was just a baby so I don't remember it—the construction almost put her out of business. But looking at this I wonder." Mostly how she made it through, but I couldn't say that part out loud.

"Oof, I don't even want to think about how much of a mess that must have been. Some of the buildings were damaged, too, I read. I guess we can be thankful we don't have scaffolding on the sides of the buildings." Marcus shrugged and I did smile then.

"Are you suggesting I need to stop with the pity party?"

"Me?" He dropped his mouth open and put a hand to his heart in mock shock before he broke the illusion with a grin.

"Ceecee, I would never tell you to put your big girl panties on and get ready for a party—especially when you know the girl that you're into is going to be there. Nope. Not me." He shook his head and I laughed.

"Fine, you big turd. But when nothing comes of this except a delivery, don't pin it on me." I pointed a finger at him, and his laughter followed me down the hall to the office.

Scooting my way inside, I was immediately back to a dark place no matter what Marcus did to drag me out of the worst corners of my mind.

My clothes were balled up in piles on top of boxes and my laundry was in a bag at the foot of my mattress squished in the back.

In this mess, I wasn't likely to find decent clothes, let alone something that I would normally wear to impress someone.

But I should probably at least try to find something that matched.

Twenty minutes later, I was dressed, wearing great boots, my hair brushed, and makeup refreshed. Even though my jeans were too tight on my behind, I still felt better about being seen in general. Clothes had magical properties. The right ones, anyway.

"Yes. Better. You look great. Now, are we taking your vehicle or mine?" Marcus asked, his eyes bright and smile wide.

Marcus didn't usually fawn over me, but he had a look where he nodded his head and his eyes widened, just shy of twinkling like he had some secret. That look was all over him right then.

I took a deep breath, my smile finally full again, and nodded.

"We have to take the van. Your car is too small, and you know it." But I tossed him the keys and went to the kitchen. He locked up while I made sure the order was secure in its packaging, and that I could keep from dropping it out of sheer nerves.

Theresa would be there, right? She and Olivia were close. But if that didn't extend to Theresa being at Carmen's birthday party, then all I could do was force Marcus take a picture of me in this outfit and hope to remember to wear it again one day.

On the way to the party, the van splashing through the soaked streets, Marcus singing along to the radio, I was stuck trying to imagine what was going to happen when we got there.

"Hello. Earth to Ceecee," Marcus said, his hand waving at me.

"Sorry, I'm just..." I didn't know how to finish that statement.

"Yeah. I know." He didn't elaborate, and I didn't ask him to.

I wasn't entirely sure I wanted to know what he thought he

knew. Especially when I was pulling into the parking lot of Joe's, and had no more time to prepare.

"Ready or not," I said, turning off the van and looking at Marcus.

"No problem. We're just going to a party. No big deal at all." Marcus nodded and climbed out.

Yep. No problem at all.

I got out of the van and tried to stick his words in my mind, keep them there and act like they were true.

"Small miracle, it's just sprinkling right now," Marcus said as we walked into the back door loaded down with the boxes of cupcakes.

"Well, Mother Nature and I had a chat. Didn't I tell you?" I asked, knocking on the door with a foot.

He laughed and a second later the door swung open.

Campbell was on the other side, his smile wide and his arms taking boxes from me before he even said hello.

"Olivia," he called into the kitchen, turning back to us and said over his shoulder. "Follow me. I'll show you where to set everything down. Was traffic bad?"

"No, everything was fine," I said, trying to remember if I even noticed the traffic around us on our way here. At least I didn't crash into anyone, because I was pretty sure I couldn't remember any of the cars we had passed.

"Hi." Olivia bounced around the corner. The general hum of talking and an occasional outburst of laughter grew louder with every step we took further into the restaurant. "You are both staying, right? I want you to meet everyone."

She was so excited, talking faster than she usually did, and there was a pink flush across the top of her nose and cheeks.

"Are you…blushing?" I asked, the words popping out before I could stop them.

Olivia bit her lip and turned back to me, her blush deepening.

We got to the dining area and the joy in the room was palpable. Whatever was making Olivia nervous, it wasn't something I could see clearly from the people around us.

Campbell set down the box he carried, kissed Olivia on the cheek, and went back to the party.

"Do you need my help to set anything up?" Olivia asked.

"No, but I do hope you tell me what has you rattled," I said, as quietly and as gently as I could.

Marcus raised his eyebrows at me and focused on laying out the cupcakes, turning to the side to pretend to give us space.

Olivia smiled and shook her head, the blush going all the way from her neckline to her hairline now.

"Well, Campbell showed his aunt an apartment tonight that he wants us to move into, and she told me I should just move in at their house so we can save money. I don't know how to say no…" She shook her head and took a deep breath, the blush finally starting to clear from her skin.

"Can you just move some things over there—not everything —and act like it's taking some time? Give yourselves a chance to find the right place to move to where you can have privacy," I said.

Marcus gave a tiny nod, still pretending he wasn't about to jump in if I gave what he considered bad advice. It was hard to keep from laughing, even though that was totally inappropriate at the moment.

She took a deep breath and smiled at me.

"Thanks, Ceecee. That might work. And thanks, Marcus, for pretending you weren't eavesdropping," she said, and then I did laugh along with them.

She was here.

Of course she was. I knew she would be, but…

I shotgunned the rest of my drink and tried to remind myself that this was fine. This was what I wanted to happen. I wanted to see her again, here, at the party.

And…nope. Didn't matter that it was all true.

My hands shook and I balled them into fists, shoving them into the pockets of my jacket.

"What in the world is wrong with you?" Katie asked, bumping into my side and staring up at me with her eyebrows knit together.

"Nothing. But, um, the cupcakes are here," I said, trying to keep my face impassive.

"Ah," Katie said, her voice a knowing chirp, a grin spreading across her face as she looked back and forth from me to Ceecee.

"So…they look yummy."

"Yeah." Ceecee looked great. I had never seen her in anything but the frilly apron from the bakery, a t-shirt and leggings. Now, though, the sweater, the jeans, the boots…if I was able to shop for her, I would have picked out those clothes. "She does - I mean - crap - no." Oh, lord, I was dying here.

Where was Deacon to run interference?

"That's what I thought. So, you were just picking on me because you were hard up for a curvy, bakery-fresh tart, huh?"

"Katie!" Someone had to save me. If I was Olivia, I would have been bright red.

As it was, I yelled so loud people around us turned to look.

"You have to shut up now. I'm working for her," I said, in a hushed voice, grabbing her shoulder and turning her to face me.

Not only was she one hundred percent wrong in why I was short with her, but this was the last conversation I wanted to have in front of most the people we knew. And I was seconds from being way more mean than last time.

"Geez, okay. Chill out. I won't say anything. I mean, unless you want me to. I will totally find out if she's into you at all. I'm good for that." She went back to smiling and bounced with a wicked gleam in her eye as she offered.

Whatever was going to happen, or not happen, between Ceecee and I, Katie was the last person I wanted getting involved. 'Subtle' wasn't a word in her vocabulary.

"Please don't. It isn't like that." It was exactly like that, but what did I have to offer her? The part wasn't even in for me to finish my work for her, and I knew she was in a tough spot and needed to focus on that.

"Theresa, you are a terrible liar, but fine. I won't meddle." She stepped back from me and whirled around, calling over her shoulder. "But I am going to meet her."

"Damn it," I muttered and stalked after her.

Katie was little, and therefore able to weave through the people milling about better than I could with my clunky brace. But no matter how much I wanted to beat her there, if I tried to run, if I shoved anyone out of the way to get there first, I would make it all worse.

Just as Katie got to the table, Ceecee, Marcus, and Olivia turned around to the rest of the dining room.

The table behind them had all the cupcakes Ceecee made, artfully arranged, and the boxes were stacked on one of the benches next to it. There was nothing left to distract them from Katie.

Crap, crap, crap, crap.

I was too damn slow.

"Theresa, hey, long time no see," Samantha said, stepping in front of me. I wrenched my knee stopping too fast to avoid running into her.

"What are you doing here?" I asked, which was not exactly polite to just blurt out, but she was supposed to be at school. And, well, I didn't want to see her.

"Oh, just back for the weekend. Needed to help my dad with something, and Deacon told me about this party." She looked me up and down, the careful, fake happy of her mask slipping in the process.

I shoved my hands back into my jacket pockets, balling up my fists.

"Yep. I'm working for my mom now. But you already knew that. Hope you have a good trip back to school," I said, stepping around her.

She grabbed my arm and tried to turn me toward her, but I couldn't turn as easy anymore. And I sure didn't want to.

"Please don't act that way. It was for the best." She looked up at me through her lashes, her lips pouting out.

The laugh just popped out of me. I couldn't help it. Because I knew that look.

"You actually thought you could come here, after what you

said to me, what you did to me, and I would what? Fall into your bed for old times' sake?"

Her mouth dropped open and she took a step back like I had slapped her.

"Samantha, you know what? You're so right." I shook my head, more at myself than at her. This was the first time I knew what I was about to say was true and I couldn't believe I hadn't seen it before. But looking past her to where Ceecee was standing, I saw it now.

"What am I right about?" Her eyes went back to trying that seductive stare thing again, all soft at the edges like I didn't have murder in mine. She even placed a hand on my arm, her touch light, like a caress through my thick jacket.

Although, honestly, she might not have even been looking at me, not really. She wasn't looking into my eyes. She was looking at her own reflection in them. I hoped she saw that I meant what I was about to say.

"It was for the best," I wrenched my arm away and kept walking toward the group of people at the cupcakes, every one of whom was nicer to me, and saw me. More than my ex ever did.

"Hi," I said, my voice almost like a sigh, and my hands loose in my pockets.

"What was Samantha doing talking to you? She needs to get back out of the state," Katie said, a sneer on her face.

"It doesn't matter. What she said tonight, and what she said when we split, it no longer matters," I said, looking at Ceecee as I spoke.

She smiled back at me. It was tentative, and it was small, but it was there.

"Are you going to stick around?" I asked, managing to sound like it was just a simple question and didn't matter one way or the other.

"You think I'm going to miss a party?" Marcus asked with a laugh and an arm slung around Ceecee's shoulders. "Come on. You two can tell me the scoop on everyone here, and point in the direction of someone who can appreciate me."

I shook my head and started back across the room with them.

"Marcus, I'm sure everyone here will appreciate you. But I don't know anyone who can keep up with you," I said.

He stood up straighter and fluttered his eyelashes like I had just made him very happy with himself while Ceecee cracked up.

The laugh that rang out from her was freer than I had ever seen her be.

It made me want to make her laugh all the time.

I still couldn't believe how well the party went. It was impossible to focus, even two days later.

But I couldn't stop trying to pinpoint the thing, the moment, I knew it went right. That Theresa liked me. And I still couldn't.

It all left me distracted and wondering if I had imagined it all.

Hopefully soon she would be back to finish her work, with the part in tow, and I would know for sure.

Would I, though? Was that even possible?

To know whether or not someone really was interested in me before I put myself out there in a way I couldn't take back was an impossible thing. But how else was I supposed to risk it?

"Ugh," I groaned, throwing away another batch of ruined dough.

At least today we had a steady stream of customers, and this was an extra batch of cinnamon rolls.

Our business for the day almost made up for taking off early the day of the party…Almost.

But the problem remained that I didn't know if the rain

would return, or if we would have enough days like that one to undo the damage of so many slow ones that had come before.

What was I thinking?

I couldn't worry about a girl.

Even if that girl was Theresa.

Not when I had so much else to think about, and far too much to do.

"Okay, Ceecee. Focus." Talking to myself in the kitchen was probably a bad sign, but I shook my hands out and squeezed my eyes shut for a second before I listened to my own advice, shut up, and got to work.

Running the recipe through my head and trying to think up new recipes, those were the only things keeping me on track.

If things kept up like that, I was going to run out of flavors to try in a month.

Oh, I hoped she wouldn't take a month.

Damn it.

Focus.

The oven dinged and I pulled out the batch of cinnamon rolls, replacing them and setting the timer again.

Pouring the icing on the fresh, hot rolls wasn't any more stimulating to my brain than making them.

Everything I did was on autopilot. And if my autopilot wasn't so practiced at what I was doing, there was a better-than-zero chance I would have poisoned someone already.

Finally, both batches were done, and I was washing my hands.

"Hi, Ceecee," Theresa's voice came from behind me. It took a moment for me to realize it was real.

"Oh," I said, turning too fast to grab the towel and dry off my hands and almost toppling over the pile of dishes stacked next to the sink. "Hi, Theresa. What's up?"

My voice was way too high. I sounded like I swallowed a tank of helium.

Settle down.

Theresa just smiled at me and held up a bag, her tool kit weighing down her other arm.

"What's that?"

"Your part came in," she said, walking toward the oven that just sat there day after day, reminding me I was running out of time to come up with a solution to all the things that needed fixed.

"That's great. I'll be right back." I chickened out and brought a tray of the new cinnamon rolls to the front, giving Marcus a dirty look as I passed him because he hadn't warned me.

Customers were still flowing in and out, and only two cinnamon rolls remained in the case from the last batch.

Even with the oven fixed, I would be behind at this rate.

I made another trip with the other tray before returning to the kitchen. And when I headed back in there again, this time to work while Theresa did, I had to take a deep breath first and prepare myself.

"Just let me know if I'm in your way," I said, getting back to work and pretending I would be able to do anything about it if I was.

"Ceecee, that's my line. If I make it hard for you to bake, just let me know. I can find something to keep me busy until you go out for another minute to help Marcus," Theresa said, her head in the oven.

How was I supposed to answer that? It was probably true, but it didn't help me.

I was screwing it up already and nothing had happened.

Maybe if I just went through the recipes again in my head.

So I did. More than once.

But the ideas wouldn't stop. Some of them were pretty good. And I wanted to write them down before I forgot.

"Can you come get me if the timer goes off? I need to go write down an idea I just had for a recipe before it leaves my brain and never returns." I waved my hand in the air next to my head and she laughed.

"No problem."

I opened my mouth to say something else and snapped it shut again, not sure what it was I even wanted to say.

Just Theresa's presence was starting to turn my brain to mush.

So, instead of talking, I fled to the front to make a note.

THERESA

Ceecee was acting odd.

Maybe it was me. Maybe spending an evening with her at the party, just walking around, talking and eating good food with our friends made me show too much of what was happening in my head.

But either way, the timer was about to go off. The numbers on it would likely count down before I would be able to limp to the office and get her.

I shoved myself up from the floor and wondered how many recipes she had in the office. Probably a million.

The front seemed busy. Marcus was probably having fun with all the people though. That guy really should have been in some high-level sales position. Like selling ice in the Arctic. He would end up President if he ever went into politics.

Knocking on the door to the office, I didn't hear any answer. Between the buzz of the people at the front, and the music playing over the speakers, I probably missed it.

I opened the door, and for a minute thought I was in the wrong room.

Stacks of boxes and bins were in every corner and on top of one was a pile of clothes.

But the desk along one wall proved this wasn't a storage closet. It was the office.

In the back was a bed squished between the filing cabinets and walls so one end was curled up because the mattress didn't fit the space.

No. Not *a* bed. Ceecee's bed.

Her clothes from the night before—including the boots— were in a heap next to the bed, proving she slept in it after the party.

We weren't drinking, so it wasn't some way to not have to drive anywhere else. It wasn't because she always had to be here so early because she said she was used to it, had done it all her life.

I shut the door and headed to the front.

Ceecee was next to Marcus, helping someone with their box of treats.

"Um, the timer," I said, not sure how I was supposed to handle the fact that I knew this thing about her that I was positive she didn't want me to know.

"Oh, thanks," she said, looking over at me before turning back to the person she was helping. She made a quick goodbye and hurried past me to the kitchen, a smile on her face.

Seconds, maybe minutes later, Marcus became aware I was still just standing there. He looked over at me, his brows high.

I smiled, or at least I tried to. Although I suspect I wasn't successful, and I had no idea how to fix my face into anything beyond the shock running through my head. So I headed back to finish my work.

Ceecee was already deftly icing the cinnamon rolls with perfect, practiced movements.

How she managed to keep going, to keep working and keep

laughing and smiling while so much fell apart that she was living in the office of the bakery, made me stop in my tracks and stare at her.

"You okay?" she asked after a moment, her hands pausing in their flawless pattern and her head cocked to the side.

This girl...She was in that place—one I couldn't imagine—and she was worried about how I was feeling?

I walked across the kitchen and straight for her.

She looked around like there was something else in this room that mattered at all, her hands still holding the icing and her face twisting into even more worry.

But the only thing she needed to worry about was if what I was about to do, what I needed to do at that moment, was something she wanted.

Making my way to her wasn't as smooth as it would have been once upon a time, and it sure as hell wasn't as cute.

Instead of my cheerleading uniform, or even cute clothes, I was in heavy duty work clothes and a thick jacket.

This girl...this girl made me not care for a minute. I just needed to know.

Finally, I stood right in front of her. Her eyes were wide and her breathing too fast.

"Ceecee," I whispered and took her face in my hands as gently as I could, my fingers running along her perfect skin.

I made sure to look her in the eye, to check and see if she was going to tell me no, but she didn't.

And I closed my eyes and leaned in, my lips touching her full, cupid's bow mouth.

She let out a little eep sound as if she was still surprised even though nothing I did was fast.

My heart hammered in my chest. I wanted to bring her out of the kitchen and keep kissing her for the rest of the day, but I couldn't push my luck.

Instead, I pulled away and looked her in the eye again.

This time, her lids were low, her gaze soft and shining.

"What was that for?" she asked, her voice so hushed I barely heard it over the music.

"Because I needed to," I said, and stepped back, although *that* wasn't what I needed. It was what we had to do.

The icing was still in her hands, the cinnamon rolls waiting, and I still had an oven to finish fixing.

"Is that okay?" I asked, begging the universe for her to tell me it was.

"Come here," she said, and leaned over to kiss me again, sending my heart hammering away in my chest again. My stomach fluttered and landed somewhere in my toes.

I didn't expect her to want me too, and I didn't want to let her go and have her change her mind.

She pulled back and gave me a smile that I wanted to see all the time, before turning back to her cinnamon rolls. She shook herself before she got back to work, sneaking a peek at me through her lashes.

"Well." I coughed into my hand and made my way to the oven to finish my own work. "What are you doing tonight?"

"Oh no." She turned to look at me, her face fallen, the corners of her beautiful mouth turned down, her eyes watery.

"What's the matter?" Did I screw it up already?

"I want to do something with you so badly, but I can't tonight. I have to do the books and ordering."

My smile was real, and just shy of laughing.

"Don't worry, Ceecee. I'll make sure we get a chance to have a date at some point."

I was singing. I couldn't help it.

She did like me. A lot.

Theresa was more than just someone doing work for me sometimes. And just in time, because she finished her work the night before.

While I baked in the early morning hours after far too little sleep—my need to take care of office stuff wasn't fake—for a few minutes it didn't matter that the bank account no longer had enough in it for me to get change if we ran out today.

Nope. The only thing that mattered for a little while was that the girl I liked, liked me back, and there was hope for a life beyond the flour dusting my hands.

My mother would have been very happy.

Knowing that made my soul soar and my singing sound better than ever.

"You know," a voice that didn't belong to Marcus said behind me, sending me whirling and flour flying everywhere.

Mr. McCarthy waved a hand in the air. It made the flour eddy around him as it fell to the floor. He looked like it was normal for him to be here at three in the morning. It most decidedly was not.

"Anyway," he said, and I looked up at the clock on the wall, sure it was wrong, "I think you could be a real singer if you wanted to. It would make more money than this place, I'm sure."

He looked around, as if this was his kitchen and he was checking that I wasn't going to set it on fire.

"Forgive me, but it's way too early for you to be here. What's going on?" I went back to working the dough, not just because I needed to get it done before we opened, but because my hands were shaking. It hid how scared and angry I was at his presence.

I didn't even get a whole day to bask in the glow of kissing Theresa without him crapping all over everything.

"Oh," he said, and laughed, as if what I said was some kind of screwed up comedy routine, "You're right that it is very early, but I wanted to let you know that today, and probably for at least a month, there will be roofers working on the building."

"Roofers?" I asked, my voice hoarse.

"Yes. They have some emergency repairs they need to make, and of course there is asbestos up there and lead paint. All that old terrible stuff that needs abated."

"Asbestos?" I couldn't seem to get out whole sentences. I just parrot words back to him.

"I'm sorry about this. But when something like this is found, I have an obligation to everyone in the building to see it's taken care of right away."

Whatever the opposite of sorry was, that was him. His eyes were narrowed, his mouth in a tight mockery of a smile, and his chin lowered.

"So," he said, twisting to look around, then waving as he turned to walk out, saying over his shoulder, "If you need anything..."

Yeah. I needed the world to stop, for time to reverse itself.

And most of all for Mom to be there to tell me what to do, how I was supposed to make this work.

Instead, I looked down at the flour on my hands, the dough on the counter, and went back to work. I did the thing my mother taught me. And I cried in the doing.

"Half measures today," I said to the empty bakery.

Or maybe I was talking to my mother's spirit.

Whatever it was I tried to appeal to, it didn't answer. There were no answers.

Today I would do half measures for all the usual items, and tomorrow…Tomorrow I would hope that I would need to make more.

Because if there were leftovers with half measures…

My hands shook as I finished laying out the dough and then washed them in the sink, pausing to watch as globules of dough fell to the stainless basin and slowly thinned until they sloughed off down the drain.

How was I supposed to pay for the bills coming due in a week?

I didn't have anything left to cut out of my budget.

As it was, I had to put the last order I placed to suppliers on a credit card that was close to maxed out. And payroll…

Going around in circles, finding things to do to keep my shaking hands busy, I filled up the remaining hours before—

Marcus whistled as he opened the back door and came inside.

For as long as he worked with me, it only took him a second to realize that the front didn't look right.

He came into the kitchen, his brows knit together, and his mouth a thin line as he took in the fact that the half-full cases were all that was on offer today.

"Ceecee, what's going on?" His voice was tentative, each word slow and deliberate, like he was defusing a bomb.

"The landlord came this morning as I was prepping," I said, sitting on a stool and staring at the twice-cleaned counter in front of me.

Marcus waited, letting me sit in this place I couldn't think a way out of. In this spot where I had to find the words.

"You came in through the alley, right?" I looked up and met his eyes as they cleared. He looked toward the back door he had walked through.

"Like always."

"Did you see the front of the building at all?"

"No."

"Come with me. I haven't had the guts to look either." I climbed from the stool, my legs didn't feel like they could move properly, but they did it.

We walked side by side. He kept glancing at me, as if he thought I would fall over at any moment.

And I might have.

Opening the front door, it was worse than I had imagined.

The door wasn't blocked, but just above our heads were massive reams of white sheeting affixed to the side of the building, wrapping all the way over the edge of the roof. And in the road, a crew was trying to erect a scaffold on the uneven cobblestones.

"Scaffolding? Was there an earthquake I missed?" Marcus asked, leaning back to look up the wall. A smattering of rain fell on his face making him squint his eyes.

"No." I tugged on his arm and ducked back inside, the cold of the day leeching into my bones, bringing shivers that wracked my body.

"What is going on out there?" He rubbed at the back of his neck and started pacing.

"McCarthy said it was asbestos and lead paint. They are

doing mitigation and then reroofing the whole thing." My throat was so dry, the last word came out as a croak.

"Oh, no, Ceecee. What do we do?"

We.

He said we.

No matter how hard I tried, I couldn't hold back the tears. They streamed down my face in a torrent of pain. The shivers running through me only got worse.

Marcus wrapped me up in a hug, patting my back with one hand and wiping his own tears away with the other.

"It's going to be okay. You can do this," he said.

Swallowing hard, I nodded and pulled away.

"I think I need to show you something." I nodded again, trying to convince myself I was doing the right thing.

He sniffed and gave me a grim smile, taking my hand.

We walked back through the bakery to the office and with my hand on the door, I bit the inside of my cheek.

It took more than a moment of just standing there to get up the nerve to open the door.

Finally, I turned the knob and showed him what was inside.

"Ceecee," he looked at me, his mouth hanging open, and back at the room, "When did this happen?"

"The first time I hired Theresa. There was no money to do it, but I had to. And all the funds I thought were extra...they paid for Mom's stone. Now there's nothing left." Telling him, getting it out in the open so someone else knew just how bad it was, loosened the tightness in my chest. But the shaking grew worse.

"How bad is this," he waved a hand in the direction of the front door, "going to be?"

I collapsed into the desk chair, leaning back with my arms wrapped around myself, fighting off the tremors running through me.

"If it goes on for more than a couple weeks, I most likely

won't make payroll. And I might not make rent, to say nothing of the other bills."

There. I said it. I admitted out loud that I couldn't afford to keep paying him, that I was going to need to let him go. And I was close to losing The Bake Place altogether.

"Don't worry about payroll," he said, crouching down next to me.

"You have bills, too. I can't do that to you." I shook my head. Seattle wasn't exactly a cheap place to live. As it was, I wasn't sure I would ever be able to find someone as good as Marcus to work here, and I didn't want him to leave me.

"Ceecee, I know you love me."

And I did. So much. I put my hand on his and squeezed.

"But you can't afford me, and I refuse to contribute to you living here. I will find something else, come and help here when I can, and when business picks up again, you can hire three people for the money you pay me."

"Marcus, I don't want to lose you." All I had left was him and the bakery.

He wrapped me up in a hug again, tighter this time, while I cried harder than before.

"You will never lose me. I don't need to be your overpaid employee to be your best friend."

Maybe I should have given it more time before I went back to try and get Ceecee to go out with me, but I didn't want to.

Maybe I should have at least gone home and changed first, but I was too excited after work.

I wanted to take her out, have fun, pretend that there was nothing going sideways in her business for a few hours. She seemed to need the break.

And I wanted to see her again.

But the construction traffic was even worse than it had been, and Pike Place was dead.

It was never dead.

At least not to the point of whole shops not being open.

Heading toward the bakery, I ran into a bunch of scaffolding lining the walls of the buildings.

"What on Earth?" I mumbled, looking up at the sheeting on the buildings and the scaffolds being erected.

This wasn't part of the construction going on, and it spanned multiple buildings. But not necessarily the ones directly next to each other. It seemed like only some of them had anything happening.

I passed the bakery the first time. It was so hard to see because the scaffolding blocked the windows, and the sign was covered by the sheeting.

"Oh, Ceecee, no." My heart ached standing outside. This would destroy her business as long as it was going on.

She didn't deserve this. Her landlord had to have plotted with some of his buddies who owned the other buildings to have all this go on at the same time.

Just suspecting it made me shove my fists into my jacket pockets.

Damn it, I needed to do something.

I walked into the bakery to find the front empty, but there were voices in the back.

"Ceecee? Marcus?" I called, not wanting to go back there if I didn't have reason.

Before, I probably would have. But now I wanted to date her. It was a different thing to barge in on someone I wanted to date.

They came out from the back, wiping their eyes and smiling. Marcus wasn't wearing an apron which made me raise an eyebrow.

"What's going on?" I asked, unsure exactly what to say because there was too much.

"I'm helping Ceecee get ready for my absence, she's suggesting places I should find a job, and the entire street is a mess," Marcus said, with a wave of his hand toward the front door.

He seemed drunk, but I didn't think either of them were. Unless they had decided day drinking was the best solution under the circumstances.

"Um, well," I looked back and forth between them and realized today was possibly the worst day ever to ask her out. "I'm planning a thing for my mom's work crew. Is it okay if I clean you out?"

Ceecee's smile went from sharp at the edges, like desperation was impersonating her, to warm and soft as she looked at me.

"See?" Marcus said, turning to look at Ceecee, "I told you that no matter what, you have people who will walk through all of that to come and buy from you. It isn't over."

While Ceecee nodded, they asked me about how many people worked for mom.

After I told them, I stood back and watched as they boxed everything up.

No matter what, some people would go out of their way to buy from her. That was true, and I bet if I called a few people, I could prove it.

"Do you remember exactly what the landlord said he was having done?" I asked, after the entire case was ready to go. Ceecee and Marcus had their coats on, ready to help me carry it all to the work truck. I was tired of speculating about how long this was going to drag on without knowing details.

"He said something about asbestos, lead paint, and a new roof," Ceecee said, piling some boxes in my arms and Marcus's before she grabbed a stack herself.

That would take a month at least. Just a guess, but we had to call in the abatement guys a while ago on a job. It delayed everything by two months because it was so extensive.

I looked up at all of it as we passed onto the customer-free street.

Somehow, I didn't think someone who was living in the office, had just fired her best friend, and looked like she was about to scream when I showed up, was going to keep her business afloat that long.

Other people called in their family when there was a prob-lem. The military in old movies called in the cavalry.

For me, I was about to call all my friends to Seattle's Best Karaoke to not sing.

This was an emergency.

But I knew, even their help was a stop gap.

What I really needed, was for Mom to come through.

"Okay, is there anything else I can do?" Marcus asked, closing the door to the office on my freshly-washed clothes.

"Not unless you can work miracles. But at least Theresa bought everything today. Now all I have to do is put these up all over and hope people listen," I said, gesturing to the signs we made and had laminated down the road.

"Well, then let's go. You tape and I'll hold." He smiled at me and picked up half the stack.

"Marcus, what are you going to do now? Have you looked at anything out there?" I grabbed my own stack and we headed out to the Market.

"There were quite a few that seemed interesting in my short little search. And I ran into my neighbor while we were doing your laundry. He said that they are looking for someone where they work. That one sounds like it would be a lot of fun."

He held one of the signs up to my existing poster on a bulletin board at the end of the street and I fumbled with my stack to get a hold on the tape.

Biting my lip, I used the tape dispenser and managed to only have a couple lumps and bubbles in it.

"There." I stood back and looked at it, wondering if making 'we're open' the biggest message on it was the right choice.

"It's great. Anyone coming this way to Pike Place should see it. It will help." He nodded, standing back and looking at it with me.

But I still wasn't sure.

I hoped.

But surety was a long way off.

We moved on to the telephone poles and our stand-up sign in the Market itself, repeating the process.

"So, tell me about this possible job your neighbor suggested."

"He works at a microbrewery. They make their own beer and are talking about expanding into distilling. But they need someone to do the tours and tastings."

Of all the things I thought he would do next, alcohol was not on my radar. It made me smile.

"That actually sounds like something you would be fantastic at. Especially if they expand. I can see you traveling all over the place and making people have so much fun while drinking that they think the booze is amazing."

Marcus laughed and bumped my shoulder, shaking his head.

But he didn't argue with me.

"At the end of all this, when your bakery is thriving, and I am setting the world on fire in some way, we will look back to right now and wonder why we were sad," he said, holding the last of the signs so I could tape it.

I tried, but the tape got stuck to itself.

Struggling to get it ripped off the dispenser without ruining the rest of the roll, tears started to drip down my cheeks.

Marcus put a hand on mine, stilling the frantic ripping movements.

"Ceecee, it's okay." He ducked his head into my vision, his face soft and his smile gentle.

"I know. But this last year is…"

What?

Too damn much?

Yes.

But it was a lot more than just that.

In the last year I lost my mom, Marcus was leaving the bakery, and I lost everything else in the process of keeping the place going.

At what point was I supposed to give in and start to think the universe was trying to tell me something?

"You're right. It has been. But that means that you're due. Something good will come of all of this. But you don't stop halfway across the trail of embers on a fire walk. You and I will keep going."

He nodded again, and this time I did too.

"Okay," I said, holding up the tape, "Let's get this done and go get a drink."

"Deal. But I'm buying, and we will be going to a movie and dinner, too. We'll just pretend it's a date and confuse everyone we meet."

I laughed out loud at that.

"Good plan."

THERESA

"Did we really need to 'drop everything and get here now'?" Katie asked, piling her hair on top of her head and tying it off.

She was cross-legged on the sofa in our usual room at Seattle's Best in her sweatpants and two layers of hoodies.

"Are you sick? I never see you in sweats," I said, momentarily distracted from my mission.

"No. I have so much homework, it's ridiculous. So, let's make this quick." She grabbed a cinnamon roll. Her eyes widened, a smile on her face, and I knew I was forgiven for pulling her away from her work, even if she wasn't going to say so.

"You're only swamped because you wait for the last minute for anything," Deacon said, around a big bite of his second roll.

"Where are Olivia and Campbell?" Katie asked, her eyes shut as she rocked from side to side, her mouth stamped in a grin.

"Good, huh?" I asked, smiling at her even though she couldn't see me, and shaking my head.

"Oh, so good," Katie cooed.

Deacon just nodded and grabbed a different treat.

Campbell opened the door and Olivia rushed in behind him, shaking the rain off her hair.

"You brought snacks." Olivia almost clapped her hands when she brought them together, bending over the boxes on the table.

"Is this all from The Bake Place?" Campbell asked, grabbing a cinnamon roll too.

They really were the most popular thing on the menu.

"Yes. And that's why I called everyone to get here right away."

I launched into the story of how bad the situation was for Ceecee and her bakery. Although I left out that she was living in her office, I did mention she had to move out of her apartment.

That seemed too personal to share, especially since I wasn't technically supposed to know that little part of the story.

Everyone stopped chewing when I mentioned that Marcus was getting another job. All of the sugar-induced happiness in the world couldn't distract my friends—the same people who dropped whatever they were doing to answer my call—from realizing how crappy it was for Ceecee and Marcus.

"Damn," Katie said, shaking her head and looking down at the half of a cinnamon roll in her hands.

"So, what do we do to help?" Deacon asked, grabbing yet another treat from a box.

"Today, nothing. Because I bought out everything she made today."

Eyebrows went up all over the room and mouths dropped open.

"All the food she made?" Campbell asked.

"Yep. It was only half what she normally does, and it wasn't nearly enough to keep her afloat. I don't think she's going to get any customers at all while all that is going on."

"Well," Olivia looked at the boxes piled on the table and down at the roll in her hand. Her mouth pinched, and a line formed between her brows. "Each of us could put in some kind of special order. Joe's could even have a special cinnamon roll added to the menu for a while, but we won't sell enough to make up all her lost revenue."

I took a deep breath. She was right, but it was all we could do until I managed to find something else.

"Right, but I bet I could add a few orders to it if I talked to coach," Deacon said, grabbing another treat.

"That would be great," I said.

"And I could spread the word on Greek row." Katie took another bite then went back to smiling.

"You guys are the best. This should help until I can get everything else in place. It isn't forever, because hopefully I can come up with a better long-term answer."

"I hope so, because even if we get her through this thing, that landlord sounds like someone who needs to be punched in the throat," Katie said, her voice hard.

Everyone laughed, but I was enjoying the picture in my head of Katie doing it. She would, too.

"What's your long-term plan, then?" Campbell asked, the only one who seemed to be slightly less distracted by the food. He looked right at me, his face open and paying attention.

I glanced at Olivia, wondering if I should say anything, because they might not be on the same page.

"Okay, so it seems clear that Ceecee needs a different location for the bakery, but space in this city is nuts." Now, I finally grabbed a cinnamon roll for myself.

"Right, so do you know any people in real estate?" Katie asked, leaning back against the couch like she was going to fall into a sweets coma.

"Sort of. My mom has agreed to give me access to my college fund money to buy a fixer upper if I work on it myself and grow the equity," I said.

Katie sat up straight, her eyes wide.

Deacon stopped eating.

Campbell froze with a bite halfway to his face.

Olivia held a hand over her open mouth.

"You're going to buy a building?"

"What?"

"She's finally giving you your money?"

"How?"

Their voices were all on top of each other in a discordant chorus, making it hard for me to tell what each of them were saying, or that really they were all saying versions of the same thing.

"No matter how shocked you all are, you can't be more surprised than my mom was." I took another bite of my cinnamon roll and stared at the boxes from the bakery.

"It's just, I only ever wanted to do one thing, and that's gone. This way, I can do something I've really been training for my whole life and do it for some good. And who knows? Maybe it can be something that works out so my mom will help me keep doing it."

Looking up at my friends, I braced myself for their reactions.

But they all looked like they were processing and not passing judgement yet.

None of them told me I had left my tools behind. None of them seemed to be thinking negative things at all.

All of them looked…supportive.

"You know, I happen to know a couple who would be more than willing to rent an apartment in a building that's still getting worked on, if there was a living space in it," Campbell said. Olivia took his hand.

"I'll put it on the list of must haves," I said with a grin.

My plan included a lot more than just an apartment for them. But I needed to find the right building to make it all happen.

"Anybody home?" A voice called from the front, and I darted out of the kitchen.

So few customers came in the door lately that only a couple things were even in the cases. But the special orders were at least keeping me busy and keeping the bills mostly paid, even if some of them were late.

It also meant the only time I spent with Theresa in the last week was at the bakery after she was done with work and while I finished things. Or when she tagged along for deliveries.

Waiting in the front of the bakery with his hands crossed behind his back and a content look on his face, Campbell studied the new cupcake duo in the case.

"Hi, Campbell. You need some cupcakes?" I asked, sliding behind the counter and smiling at him.

"Not unless you have flan cupcakes, because that would combine my favorite desert with a cupcake and...even I wouldn't be able to turn that down."

Campbell laughed, but I cocked my head to the side. The

possible ways I could make that concoction ran through my head.

"You know, I bet I could make that happen," I said, leaning on the counter.

"Really? When you get that recipe ready, let me know." His smile was huge.

"So what brings you all the way down here? Something special for Olivia?"

"Actually, this is for the pool hall I teach classes at sometimes." He moved his hands to the front and I realized how long his fingers were.

"How did I not know you teach people how to play pool?"

"It's only sometimes. I spend most of my time at Joe's working. But I love playing and this is a way to do that. It was Olivia's idea."

Every time he said her name, his mouth turned up in the smallest of smiles, even when he wasn't talking about something that would necessarily warrant smiling.

"You two are relationship goals," I said, and then bit my lip.

"Sorry, I didn't mean to say that out loud."

He laughed and shook his head.

"And you and Theresa? How's that going?"

Now it was my turn to smile for no real reason.

Campbell's smile grew in response.

"That good, huh?" he asked, leaning on the other side of the case.

"Well, she's…I don't know." I shook my head. The words just swirled around in my head instead of lining up into anything resembling a coherent thought.

"Yeah, I say the same thing about Olivia." He shook his head and stared off into space, that smile telling me more than a whole soliloquy.

"Theresa told me that she and Olivia dated right before you

two met, is that true?" I asked, wondering if he was going to be upset by the question.

"Olivia and I met right after they broke up, but they were both ready to move on. I'll tell you the whole story of Olivia and I getting together sometime. That was when Theresa started dating Samantha." He shook his head, his mouth twisting to the side.

"I still can't believe she did that to Theresa. It's just so crappy. Wasn't she at the party at Joe's?" And wasn't inviting her a terrible decision?

"Yeah. That turned out to be a mistake. But at least Theresa knows she's completely over Samantha now."

He put his hands on the counter right in front of me and stared into my eyes.

I leaned back, not sure what he was doing and more than a little tempted to step all the way back.

"Are you going to treat my friend better than that?" he asked.

"Oh," I said, relaxing. This was a totally okay reason to look so intense. "Yes. No matter what happens, I will treat her better than that."

"Good then. Okay, so are you ready to take my order now?" Campbell asked, stepping back and grinning.

I laughed and grabbed my pen and notebook.

"Are you sure you want to go this far to look at a building?" Mom asked, navigating around a box truck parked in the middle of the road with its back door all the way open and nothing in the cargo area.

"The building in Queen Anne—"

"Was a ridiculous price for a tear down," Mom interrupted.

"Right, it won't work, and one of the only other ones I think might work based on the specs is down here."

Mom made a 'hmph' sound, still not buying into this as even a remote possibility.

And, if I was being honest with myself, I wouldn't have even looked in Alki if it wasn't for the gnawing desperation and need to make this happen.

Chances were high that Olivia and Campbell wouldn't want to live this far away from Joe's when they were used to being walking distance or less away. Olivia lived upstairs from the restaurant for heaven's sakes.

I rubbed at my forehead, trying to think of something I had

missed, some way to make this process faster and more likely to work.

"Okay, I think this is it," she said, looking up at the large brick building in front of us.

"Well, it looks better than the last one," I said.

That 'hmph' noise came out of Mom again as she parked the car along the curb.

"Do you have someone meeting us here?" she asked as we climbed out and looked up at the three-story building.

"Yeah. They should be here any second."

As I finished the sentence, a tiny blonde woman in an outfit I associated with ski resorts and not downtown Seattle, walked out of a large door on the ground floor and waved.

"Halloo. Are you Theresa?" she asked, looking at Mom.

Great. Another one.

"Did she really say, 'Halloo?'" Mom grumbled.

"I'm Theresa," I called, limping my way across what used to be a parking lot, but was now just shards of shattered concrete with mounds of dirt and far too many blackberries sprouting from it.

"Oh." She cocked her head to the side and her smile fell.

"Again?" Mom asked, turning to look at me as I sighed.

"Always, Mom. Always."

Mom straightened up and her face fell into that, I will kill you and make it look like an accident look, that quelled even the biggest swaggering misogynist on any of our jobs. That look made her a success.

"Do you have the paperwork I asked for?" I asked, making it clear to them both I wasn't about to stand here and play a game of 'Is She Old Enough and Qualified Enough for This Property.' We played the same stupid game at every single place we had seen so far.

"You know, this property will be a lot of work. Are you sure it's what you're looking for? I mean, the parking lot alone—" the realtor started, the same as the other ones.

"The parking lot is what? Fifty car capacity?" I asked.

She looked back and forth between me and Mom and then down at the papers in her hand.

"It's, um, about 8500 square feet. So close to that depending on how you lay it out," the realtor said, sounding awed and even suspicious.

"Less than three hundred and fifty yards of concrete for the slab. No big deal. I've budgeted for more than that." I raised a brow at her and waited while she realized that the person who needed to question themselves here was not me.

"Okay. Um, here are all the papers you requested." She handed over the entire folder she had, even though I was sure there was something in there that was part of her notes and had nothing to do with what I needed.

"How does the foundation look?" Mom said, leaning over my shoulder to look at the reports from the city and the last information from the previous owner.

"Well, this says they did work on it twenty years ago." I pointed and she read, making that noise again.

But this time I agreed with her noise.

"Let's go see," I said, walking past the realtor who looked like she wasn't sure whether she should follow or not.

She could stay outside. We were more than capable of assessing the building on our own.

Mom stopped in the entryway, looking around at what once had probably been a decent space. Now it was narrow and chopped up into a maze of dark hallways with peeling wallpaper.

"This will all need to be changed," Mom muttered, and I could see the tally of costs happening in her head.

It was happening in mine, too.

But more than that, I was trying to calculate how long it would take me just to get the main floor, the business floor, usable.

Maybe too long.

"Come on, there's no reason to look at the rest until we check out the foundation," I said, and Mom nodded.

I went around to the back of the stairs, taking two wrong turns through doors off the strange halls.

Finally, I opened a door and found the stairway down, but when I flipped on the light nothing happened.

"Not great. No power," I said.

Mom pulled out her flashlight and shined it down the stairs to what looked like a black abyss.

"Why does it look so shallow? There's only six steps." I leaned forward, trying to understand what I was seeing.

"It's full of water," Mom said.

"Oh, no."

The second she said it, I saw it. The water was thick with grossness impenetrable to the light in her hand.

"Sorry, Theresa, I don't think this is something you want to take on."

Mom was right, but it still sucked.

Foundation problems were always the biggest worry, because the issue could be so large that the building wasn't safe until it was fixed, especially in a city prone to small earthquakes.

But this was next level bad.

Seattle was far too wet, and most of it was basically landfill on top of the shallows of the ocean. Water in a basement, eating away at the concrete every second it was down there, while covering up the damage it was doing in the process, made giant question marks in my head. And it was a problem I had never been forced to learn how to mitigate. Which made this place in need of too big of a fix for my timeline.

"Damn," I said, shutting the door and heading back outside.

The realtor was still and silent, almost shocked, when I handed her the papers and walked past, Mom right along with me.

Once we were back in the car and pulling away, Mom looked at me and asked, "Is there a reason you're only looking at commercial spaces?"

"Because the price of single-family homes big enough for what I need would be astronomical, even if it was in bad shape." I slumped down in my seat, biting on my lower lip and tried to think past the problem.

"Maybe, but why not open up the search to anything with the square footage and land you think you'll need."

I looked over at Mom and tried to figure out how I could have been so stupid.

"Hey, I didn't think I was going to be able to find you," I said, handing the box to Katie as she jumped up and down in excitement.

"Yay! I'm so glad you did. Come on in," she said, stepping back from the door of her dorm room.

"Don't your dads live right by? Why do you live in the dorms?" I took a seat on a couch up against one wall while she put the box on the desk. She took one of the cinnamon rolls out and took a bite before she answered.

"Yeah, and I love them. But would you want to answer questions when you roll in at four in the morning? Or every time you bring a date home?" She shook her head and then took another bite of her roll, her eyes closing as she sunk into the desk chair.

"Well, I want to thank you for telling Greek row about the bakery. They seem to put in an order every day from one house or another."

And it was true, even though she waved a hand like it was nothing.

Greek row's orders gave me a lot of running around to do on the weekends. And that helped a lot, but during the week I was still struggling to make even a quarter of what a regular day had been before.

Katie didn't need to know that. She was helping and I appreciated it. That's what she needed to know.

"So, tell me about you and Theresa. I need to know everything," Katie said, leaning forward and taking another bite of her roll.

But this time her eyes were wide and sharp and her smile more wicked than sweet.

"I don't know what all there is to say. She's great, and we're figuring it out while it's kind of tough right now."

How much did she and Theresa talk about our relationship?

The answer didn't seem to be forthcoming as she just stared at me, looking vaguely predatory.

It took an act of will to suppress the need to fidget while she looked at me.

"Well, I'm glad you two are together," she said after a prolonged silence as she leaned back in her chair finally and let me take a breath.

"Um, thanks, Katie."

Answering when someone said that was always weird. Even with her. What was I supposed to say, I wasn't glad? Of course I was. Just weird.

"Especially because she made Olivia order all those cinnamon rolls for Joe's, so now I can get one every time I go eat there." She laughed and went on talking and eating, seemingly unaware that her words had frozen me to the spot.

Olivia only ordered all those cinnamon rolls daily because Theresa told her to?

I thought that she did it because she thought they were great and would be a good addition to the menu at Joe's, not because my girlfriend thought I was a charity case she needed to save.

They thought I couldn't do it on my own, that I needed their handouts.

Did Theresa even really like me, or did she just feel sorry for me?

After she was finished with her cinnamon roll, I stood up and excused myself, pretending I had a lot of work to do.

But what I needed to do was get out of there.

Tears of sheer frustration pressed at the back of my eyes so hard it was difficult to hit the right button on the elevator.

I took deep breaths, sucking down the air. It was flavored with stale popcorn and what I suspected was old pot smoke.

College never sounded like something I wanted, but the people I passed as I walked out of the dorm toward the parking lot just seemed so free.

None of them worried that their girlfriends only dated them out of pity and a weird desire to save someone.

All of them probably dated lots of people in their classes, or had random hookups. Some of them were probably in love.

While I was in some limbo place.

My beautiful, cheerleader girlfriend—who was always out of my league—felt bad for the poor, overworked girl who couldn't manage without her mother.

Except that wasn't true.

I was going to do just fine without her.

The parking lot seemed like it was a million miles away from the dorm. By the time I got there I was out of breath and a cramp in my hamstring made me want to deal with it tomorrow.

But it couldn't wait.

I couldn't wait.

I thought about just texting her, but I wasn't going to be

talked about as the kind of person who broke up with someone via text.

That was cowardly.

She picked up on the third ring.

"Hi, Ceecee. How are your deliveries going?"

While I still wanted to tell her where to shove it, hearing her voice made me double over in the seat and press my forehead to the steering wheel.

"You know, I could have helped you. It must have taken forever to get across campus with that box for Katie."

"Could have helped me? What, limped along next to me?" I snapped and banged my head against the steering wheel. That was crossing the line.

"Uh," she mumbled, and cleared her throat.

"I'm sorry. That was uncalled for and unfair. But you don't need to help me with anything anymore. I know what you've been doing." I talked so fast it was hard for even me to be sure if I was speaking clearly, but I had to get this over with.

"What are you talking about?" Her voice was hard, angry, and all it did was piss me off.

"You tried to step in and take over like I can't do anything on my own. I have connections. I have been running this business all by myself since my mom died. Were you there when she passed? Did you organize her funeral while doing everything? Did you manage all the debt getting called in at once because she was dead? Did you? No."

"Ceecee," she yelled, in a shocked voice.

"Don't call me again, Theresa. Don't come to the bakery. If you feel the need to get something from me then you can go to one of your little minions who have played your game. Good-bye, Theresa."

I hung up the phone and dropped my head down to the steering wheel again.

At the end I wasn't even making sense, but it didn't matter. I did what needed to be done.

The right thing to do for the business, for Mom's legacy, was to focus on work anyway.

"Yeah. The right…" I sniffed and swiped at the tears running down my cheeks. "I did the right thing."

And it felt like the worst.

"*D*amn it, what?" I yelled into the phone, but the call was done.

"Ceecee. Ceecee pick up," I said as I called her back, but it cut off. Dialing again just sent it straight to voicemail.

"She blocked me. Why? What the hell was that?" I yelled, turning to Deacon who sat across the table from me with his cards squished in his large hands like he squeezed them to death while I was getting my heart shredded.

"I don't know, Theresa, but are you okay?" He looked like he wasn't okay for me, which was good because I didn't know what to feel.

"How am I supposed to be okay or not when I don't even know what just happened?" I threw my phone onto the cushion of the couch.

It bounced off but managed to land on the ottoman anyway.

"See? I almost broke my stupid," I picked up my cards and threw them too, sending them fluttering around the room, "phone."

"Theresa." Deacon shook his head and put his cards down.

"No, don't try and make me feel better, Deek. She just broke up with me. She…"

And it happened. No matter how confused I was, or how much I hated doing it, my body caught up to what was going on before my brain fully did, and I started to cry.

"Deacon. I tried. After Sam and everything that happened, I didn't want to, but I tried." I crumpled onto the table, putting my head in my arms.

"Just because you had a fight, doesn't mean it isn't worth it to keep trying," he said, putting one of those huge hands on mine.

"No, Deek. We didn't have a fight." I lifted my head from my arms. Even in the warmth of the room, the air hitting my soaked cheeks sent a chill down my body. "She broke up with me. It's over. It didn't matter how hard I tried. She said I tried to save her, and she could do it herself."

"Stop it. This isn't about something you did wrong or something you didn't do. This sounds like it was about her." He shook his head, his mouth setting into a thin line.

"Deacon, it doesn't matter if I try or not. It doesn't matter if the bad things that happen are my fault or not. I end up by myself and all alone."

He squeezed my hand hard, his mouth turning down. His face looked close to what I assumed it must have when he was on the football field.

I sat up straight and tried to pull my hand away, but his grip was too tight.

"You are not alone. And I never want to hear you say that again," he said, his voice low and almost growling.

"Geez. What happened to Deacon of the Too Pure?" I grumbled, but the tears stopped.

"There. That's better." He smiled and let go of my hand, giving it a little pat.

"Seriously, you're kind of scary when you want to be."

"Well, I can't be sunshine and rainbows when I need to flatten people for my team."

Huh. That actually made so much sense it shocked me the rest of the way out of the crying part of the pity party.

I took a deep breath and slumped in my chair, rubbing my face and swiping my hair out of the tracks of tears on my cheeks.

"Fine, I get it. I have you and the others. But, damn it, I wanted her too."

Not all of the pity party was over.

"You know that she's just in a messed-up situation. I mean, she really is about to lose everything." He shook his head, his face back to the soft, sweet look of one of my best friends.

"The bakery," I said, feeling the hurt for her over the struggle of her business.

"Her apartment."

"She had to fire Marcus."

"And she already lost her mom," Deacon said, nodding.

"But then why is she pushing me away because I'm trying to help, to take some of the burden?" I yelled, throwing my hands up.

"Let me ask you something." He put his hands flat on the table like he was bracing himself. I braced myself in turn, crossing my arms over my chest.

"If you get a building like you want to, if you find the perfect one and get her to move in and all the rest, but you start to struggle under the weight of the task and fail to make it work, would you accept your mom swooping in to help?"

"That's not...I..." I turned to the side and looked out the window, the grip of my fingers on my arms slowly loosening until my hands dropped into my lap.

"Oh, no," I said, laying my forehead down on the table.

"Right," Deacon said, leaning back.

"Where does that leave me?" I asked, lifting my head from the table just enough to make eye contact.

"I would say, keep looking. Let her figure herself out."

Sitting up the rest of the way, I opened my mouth to argue. That didn't make sense.

"Theresa, wait, I wasn't done," he said with a smile and a hand raised in the air like he was a little kid at school who had the answer.

"Okay, I'm going to listen to all of it and not interrupt." I nodded at him and tried to do as I promised.

"Well," he said, pausing to lean a little forward like he was about to impart the secret of the universe and getting me close to laughing even under the circumstances, "You need to keep going. You need to find a place, start working on it, do what you can, and wait. While you do all of that, she will be stuck in that same crappy situation and thinking. No one is there with her. All she has is time to think and to second guess."

"Nightmare."

"Yes. And then you set up a situation where she goes to see a new space for the bakery—let's say she goes with Marcus or with Campbell. And then you tell her you've been doing this and that you want her back." He leaned back, very happy with himself with a grin on his face.

"Deacon you're a genius," I said, shaking my head.

"I know."

But what if…what if she didn't want to try again? What if I didn't?

Looking down at my own hands, the callouses on them, I decided that even if she and I didn't end up together, it was still a good thing to help her with the business. In the way that only I could.

"Okay," I said.

CEECEE

My hands didn't want to stop shaking.

The only time I felt like I was really functioning anymore was when I was baking. But I didn't have any foot traffic, and the orders weren't enough to keep me busy all day.

So, I was back in my pajamas, laying in my broken-down bed, staring at the desk and the pile of paperwork on it after delivering what little I needed to on a Wednesday.

I was late on three bills.

Even though I had the money to do it, the energy to tackle them remained deep inside my body, hidden behind the shaking of my hands.

Marcus was out of town, taking the chance for a vacation while he waited to start working at his new job. Plus, he still needed to finish trying all of their options and reading through the pile of material they sent him about beer.

Not even Marcus was around to distract me from the ever-shrinking walls.

It wasn't like I had a television to zone out to.

Even if I did, I wouldn't have been able to afford any service for it. Cable was way too expensive, and I didn't have internet other than my phone. That was the cheapest plan, and I was afraid I would run out of data.

That stupid phone was the only thing that brought in any money from the orders.

Sure, I could do it all myself.

Wasn't that what I told Theresa?

I was an idiot.

Maybe I could have done it all myself if there was any capital to pay for advertising, but I was barely keeping myself afloat well enough to start putting some money away. I wasn't paying anything but the minimum on the debts.

All the lights in the bakery were off. Just like they had been for a week unless I was in the kitchen working.

The heat was down to fifty degrees, and I wore layers all the time to keep warm.

But I was surviving, even if it was only barely.

I needed to use the bathroom.

For some reason though, the thought of getting up and walking there made me want to just roll over and try to go to sleep.

It was a lot of work.

No one cared if I exerted the effort. Most people didn't care whether I worked at all. So why couldn't I just lay in bed all day?

My bladder told me that it cared and wasn't going to let me sleep no matter what I tried to tell it.

Finally, I threw my blankets off, wrapped my robe tighter against the chill that flooded me the second I stood up, put my feet into my slippers, and shuffled my way to the bathroom.

After I was done, I went to flush, and all the water disappeared just like it was supposed to. But the tank didn't fill again.

"Damn it. Come on," I muttered, looking for the same thing

that had happened before, but there was no water on the floor and the fix Theresa did seemed to be fine.

"What in the hell?" I straightened up and tried the sink.

But no water came out there either.

I rubbed my hands over my face and spent ten minutes swearing while I put on something that more closely resembled clothing.

The perfect person to call was Theresa. This was exactly what she said might happen. Something with the water.

But there was zero chance I was going to call her.

Nope. That ship was long out to sea, and I was the one who gave it the wind to get there.

The neighbors gave me contact info for a few contractors back when Mom was alive.

Maybe one of them could help me.

Only one of them picked up. He agreed to come out, saying he had time to look at it real quick.

I had no idea what looking at it 'real quick' would do for me, but it was the only chance I had.

He took an hour.

That wasn't quick, real or otherwise, but I didn't complain.

"Cold in here," he said, walking back out to the front of the shop.

"Because of the construction I close down early," I said, which was only partially a lie.

"Yeah, it seems like a lot is happening here. And I hate to tell you this, but more work needs to be done." He shrugged and shook his head before he went on. "I think your whole plumbing system needs to be replaced. I suspect none of the units are separated properly which didn't help this old set up. I find it more often than you think. Parts of a system are updated, others aren't. And the whole time none of them are separated or done properly."

"The whole…" I couldn't finish the sentence. There weren't words for how bad this was. There weren't words that would allow me to tell this perfect stranger that he just killed me.

"Ceecee?" Mr. McCarthy came in the front door with his face white and his jowls shaking.

"Yes?" I asked while I silently begged the contractor not to say anything.

"I just got a call from upstairs that there's no water," Mr. McCarthy paced across the front of the store, apparently not noticing that the heater was so low or that the cases were empty.

"Well, I was just telling her it's because the entire plumbing system in this old building needs to be replaced." The contractor turned to look at Mr. McCarthy, who stopped pacing and looked the contractor up and down.

"Did you hire a handyman?" Mr. McCarthy asked, looking at me.

"First of all, I am a licensed and bonded contractor, not a random handyman. And second, I'm just here to give her a quote," he said, nodding his head once.

My heart hammered in my chest, and I wrapped my shaking hands together, holding them against my chest.

"Ceecee," Mr. McCarthy said, turning to look at me again, "We need to talk."

THERESA

"*D*o you realize how close this is to Joe's?" I asked, leaning forward in the car, straining against the seatbelt, trying to see further up the street.

"Sit back," Mom said, shaking her head.

I did what she asked, but it was hard to contain how excited I was.

"And we don't know if it has parking…what exactly the square footage is…anything?" I asked for the tenth time since she told me about a building one of our clients told her about.

"No. I know as much as you do—the address and that one of our clients thinks I could do something with it. What that means, I have no idea."

We turned a corner and I realized we were one block over from Joe's. If I had a path in a straight line, it would have taken me maximum five minutes to walk there.

Mom looked at the address on her phone's GPS and pulled over, parking on the street in front of what looked like a weird set up for a house.

I got out of the car and stared up at the building.

"Four stories?" I asked looking at the dormers in the top with large enough windows for there to be rooms up there.

"Actually," she said, pointing to one side of the building where the hill dipped to reveal a door in the foundation, "I think it's five."

"Holy crap." I started toward the place, trying to figure out what it was once upon a time.

It was old. Some of the ornate gingerbread details in the gables and around the windows and doors made it clear that it was more than just a dilapidated building.

This was an old girl who was still standing stronger than some newer buildings we had toured. Even if she had been neglected.

I liked her. In my mind I could see what she would look like after some proper love. The gingerbread gave me a detail to build off of. It might be extra work, more than might, it was. But repairing that and finding more in a salvage yard or having some made would give her a grand touch.

"Wow," I said, and Mom nodded.

"You know, if you cleared out this front yard, there should be room for a couple dozen parking spots," she said, looking down the fence and across to the other, probably doing better measurements in her head than most people did with a measuring tape.

"I wonder if it has alley access and a backyard, too." I headed around to the back with Mom at my heels. The exposed portion of the foundation—the whole side with the door and a few windows—looked sound at first glance.

The backyard wasn't nearly as big as the front, but it existed. There was even a small strip of gravel carved out of the yard like it was used for parking with a garage at one end. While the garage was intact, it listed slightly to the right. Most likely it didn't have the proper framing and support along the walls.

Not a big deal to fix so far.

"We should look in that garage. There's no door," Mom said, not waiting to see if I would follow her. She knew I would.

I expected to see a lot of things inside the building after being wide open to whoever for however long, but I did not expect to see a the pile of lumber that reached up to the rafters.

"That's dimensional. That's usable," I said. Mom nodded, her mouth open.

"How much is this place going for?" I asked.

She turned to give me a pointed look with her mouth pinched.

"Let's just look at the whole property first, shall we?" She turned around and headed to the main building.

"Am I going to have to shimmy in through a cracked window?" I asked as we came to the basement.

"No, they gave me the key." She shook her head at me and unlocked the door which looked like a cheap metal one from decades ago.

Inside the basement, we both took out our flashlights and turned them on.

"Holy crap." I wandered through the large open basement, supported by thick posts at all the right places.

Toward the back there was a laundry room, a bathroom, and the stairs heading up.

I didn't wait for Mom. I just went up the stairs to the main floor.

I knew by the time we were done that not only was there space for a bakery, a pool hall, and apartments, but there was also room for two other things—one of which would work as space for me as I slowly redid it all.

"Do you really think it's livable right now?" I asked, leaning against the world's ugliest goldenrod stove.

"Yeah, it's nicer than the place I brought you home to when

you were born. You need to do a lot of work, and prioritize the spaces that will bring in the most money first. But replace all the appliances, do a thorough scrub, and you can for sure move in while you do the work."

"And you really want to invest in this idea? Even though this is a long-term investment, not quick flip?"

"Theresa, I think that if you do this, slowly, overtime, while you do a flip a year for me, this will be well worth the investment. Especially since I know there will be very little vacancy between you and all your friends. And since I know that you're putting all your money on the line, too."

I looked around me at the apartment in the attic. It was only partially finished into an incredibly outdated one bedroom, but if I finished it all, and did a ton of updates, there could be three bedrooms.

Three bedrooms, two bathrooms, with an incredible view over the rooftops of most of the buildings nearby...in the very top apartment.

Somewhere along the way, I went from avoiding all stairs if I could, to wanting this place, no matter how many stairs it took me to get up here.

Yes. I was investing all of my money in this.

And it was perfect.

"Let's go sign the papers," I said.

CEECEE

The contractor was gone. Watching his back go through the door, I wanted to snatch him back and beg him not to leave me alone with Mr. McCarthy.

But I didn't do any of that. Instead, I just stood there wringing my hands together against my chest and trying not to burst into tears.

"Did you know there is a health code that says any place that serves food must have water?" Mr. McCarthy asked a few moments after the contractor was gone.

"No." Lie. I did know that, but I wasn't going to admit it to him. No matter what I said, I knew he was going to do the same thing to me regardless.

"Well, I'm very sorry Ceecee. I must shut you down. And because of all the work that must be done here, I'm afraid I need you to vacate the premises." He smiled and held his hands out to the side as if to say, what are you going to do?

"But…" But what? I didn't have anything to follow that up with. Not when I knew he was going to do this the first chance he got. I couldn't even ask him to pay me back for the last time I had Theresa work on the water.

He couldn't know I hid it all from him. Especially not now that he had a large bill on his hands that he could probably try to force me to pay.

"I'm very sorry. And tell you what, because you have been such a wonderful tenant all these years, and in the memory of your mother, I'm going to give you a week to remove all your things. I'm sure you have many office and kitchen items you'll need in your next space. Bye now."

McCarthy waved a hand over his head as he walked out the door, letting it close behind him without looking back at the disaster he left.

Well, if I was going to be out of here in a week and he was going to be on the hook for the last power bill since workers would be in here, then I was going to make the most of it.

I went from living in the dark to having the lights on all the time and the heat up to seventy-five.

But even at that temperature, I spent the rest of the day cold and in bed.

After a night of almost no sleep, I heard the chime above the front door and hauled myself out of bed to tell them to go away.

Campbell stood in front of the counter looking at the cases with a confused expression on his face.

"Are you really not making anything for these right now?" he asked, pointing to the cases as I got to the counter and leaned on it.

"Nope. Why would I do that when I'm supposed to be out of this shop in six days?"

His mouth dropped open and he pinched his whole face together. He looked like he had been shot.

"I'm sorry, Ceecee. That's terrible. Now I know why you

weren't at Joe's this morning with the cinnamon rolls." He shook his head.

"Yep. No desire to bake at this moment. I should really call all my orders and cancel them," I said, although it sounded just as devoid of feeling as the rest of my words. I couldn't imagine getting the energy together to actually do it.

"Ceecee, I wasn't going to say anything because I know you're attached to this place, but I think I know a great place for the bakery."

"Wait, what? No, I'm not attached to the building. I'm attached to The Bake Place." I stood up straighter. I actually wanted to go out and see what he was talking about instead of staying in bed all day again.

"Oh, great, because it's right by Joe's. I can show you if you want," he said, stepping away from the counter like he thought I was going to follow him out the door in my pajamas.

As much as I wanted to go that second, I did need to ditch the pj's.

"Perfect. Wait right here. I just need to get dressed real quick." I darted back to the office and changed my clothes in record time, throwing my hair up in a messy bun and adding another sweater.

I locked the back door and followed Campbell out the front, locking it too.

We made our way through the Market to where Campbell was parked and headed toward Olivia's restaurant.

"You weren't kidding when you said it's right by Joe's. We could walk there," I said, climbing out of his car.

The building looked a little tired and much older than I expected, but there was a charm to it.

In the front, a few guys were laying out gravel over well-flattened ground like they were about to turn it into a parking lot.

Fantastic, because I had never had my own parking lot. Not one day while I was in business, nor in all the years my mom was before me could we rely on having a parking lot.

We walked up to a large, gorgeous, front door with sidelights and a transom.

Campbell got there first and opened the door for me.

"Oh, thanks," I said, stepping through and holding it open for him in return.

But he shoved my arm away from the door and yanked it shut, pulling out a key and locking it a moment later.

"Hey. What are you doing?" I asked, genuinely confused, because Campbell was never even rude, let alone hostile or a prankster.

"Look at the floor," he yelled then mouthed, "Sorry," before he turned and walked away.

"What the hell?"

But I looked down at the floor like he said. There were rose petals strewn all along the front hall and heading off to the left through a set of French doors.

Part of me wanted to go another way, to get out and run as far and as fast as possible.

Not only was I not sure I could handle facing the person I was sure was on the other side of those doors, but I looked terrible. Tears already threatened the backs of my eyes.

But I took a few steps. Then a few more. I even managed to open the glass doors. On the other side, sitting at a little bistro table in the middle of a large room with gorgeous wood floors and three brand new ovens sitting around for no reason, Theresa held a rose and smiled at me.

"Hi, Ceecee."

I broke down in wracking sobs and lurched my way to her, throwing my arms around her neck and kneeling in front of her.

"Theresa, I'm so sorry. And I'm so stupid."

"But you're here now," she said, bending her face to mine and giving me the sweetest kiss. One I had missed more than I even realized before that moment.

"Are you sure you want that one?" I asked, cocking my head to the side and assessing the pale pink swatch Ceecee chose for the walls in the bakery.

"Yes. I'm sure. You know, I know my bakery pretty well," she said, shaking her head, giving me a kiss, and turning back to the phone in her hand.

I grabbed her hand and tugged her back around to me, kissing her again.

She made that little eep sound I loved, and I deepened the kiss, reaching up to thread my fingers through her hair at the nape of her neck where it was soft and fine as silk.

Her hand gripped the lapel of my jacket and she leaned into me, her softness starting to melt against me and making me want to haul her back upstairs.

Then her phone chimed, and she smiled against my mouth before pulling back from me.

While I didn't want to let her go, I just sighed and decided I was going to order dinner later so we would have more time for kissing.

"But your bakery is different now. You renamed the special order portion Queen of The Bake Place. You could do whatever you want with it," I said, trying to get her attention back from the conversation with Marcus.

All I accomplished was getting a wave of the hand.

Ceecee expanded the bakery's offerings to include far more cupcakes and treats.

Her special order side of the business was already up and running in one of the two extra spaces which we turned into a kitchen, and the computer she ran her website through for her orders was in my space.

My cupcake queen was busy.

But that was okay. It made us a lot of money now that all she did was bake. She had a staff to do the rest, including the hapless guy who once an hour came into my space to check the website.

Somehow, I needed to get the office in the bakery done soon so she could at least move that guy in there.

My to do list was long.

We planned on surprising Campbell with the next finished space just for him.

It was tough working on it in secret while he and Olivia lived in the building in their own dated apartment. Although Carmen gave them the ugliest couches in history that used to be in her basement and they just embraced the gross side of the seventies until I got around to remodeling their floor.

But I worked on his special space while he was at work, and the bakery while he was home.

Both spaces were almost ready.

That would be the main floor done, the basement done, the second floor rented to Campbell and Olivia, Ceecee and I on the fourth, and I still needed to get the third-floor apartment ready to rent out. It was in the worst shape.

After that, I would finally be able to redo Olivia and Campbell's apartment and then our own. Of course, all of that was around the other work I had to do for my mom.

Ceecee and I had already planned what we would do.

While I hadn't had the time to turn it into my full vision, it was still a nice enough apartment. Although that was mostly due to who I shared it with.

Mom kept me pretty busy with her flips, and I was plenty busy doing my own version of a flip here. But watching Ceecee wander through my workspace, running a hand along all the tools and supplies piled up all over the place, I realized it was right where I needed to be.

"Are you really not going to show me the finished product before Campbell sees it?" I asked, sitting on the couch with Theresa's leg slung across my lap while I rubbed her knee.

The scars that crisscrossed it were too tight in some places, so I rubbed them almost every day with vitamin E oil and she pretended I never accidentally hurt her. But she was walking better already, and making her way up and down the stairs didn't mean she had to take a break part way up and anymore.

"Sweet, you won't let me surprise you with anything I'm doing in the bakery. Let me surprise you with this," she said, tilting her head up from the arm of the couch to look at me, her smile soft.

"Did you just call me, Sweet?" I asked, the look on her face and the new nickname making all the butterflies in the world fly around in my stomach.

Managing to do it without removing her leg from my hands, or even jostling me, Theresa sat up and cupped my face in her hand, staring into my eyes.

"Ceecee, I want to call you something that only I say, so every time you hear it, you know I'm actually saying I love you." Theresa's voice was soft, but nothing about her was hiding.

Did she just say she loves me?

She did.

My chest rose and fell in frantic breaths, and I couldn't get the words out fast enough.

"I love you, too," I said.

Theresa closed her eyes, peace falling over her features as she smiled and pressed her forehead to mine.

Our hands found each other, our fingers intertwining. I never wanted to let her go.

Her phone chimed and she growled, opening her eyes right in front of mine, her forehead still against mine.

I laughed and pulled back.

She grabbed her phone and swung her legs down.

"Come on, it's time for you to be surprised by Campbell's space." She strapped her brace back on her knee.

"Wait, now? And Tee, why don't we put in an elevator? It would save your knee." I scooted forward, managing to contain the bouncing I wanted to do.

"Don't think I'm not trying to figure out how to make an elevator happen." She smiled, finishing up the strap on her brace, but the smile softened. "And yes, now, but…" She turned back to me and kissed me, making me want to tell her that I never wanted to see his space if it meant stopping this kiss.

Theresa pulled back with another growl, rubbing a thumb over my bottom lip.

"Olivia and Campbell are going to be here in ten minutes, and the sign went up today so we're starting outside. But I want more time," she said.

It didn't matter how many times Theresa, this beautiful woman, said something like that to me, it never failed to send my heart into overtime and make everything about the world better.

But we had to go celebrate with our friends.

And I couldn't wait to see what she had accomplished.

"Let's go see The Shark," I said, giving her a quick kiss and pulling her to her feet, "We have lots of time."

Thank you for reading!

If you enjoyed this book, please leave a review at your favorite bookseller.

Don't forget to go to darleneeverly.com and sign up for the newsletter to be the first to know when the next Comfort Food romance makes it to the table.

The next book in the series, Brewed Anew will be coming in February 2022 and the first book in the series, Personal Pan is available now!

ACKNOWLEDGMENTS

A whole hearted thank you to Bean, the Rottens, and all of my friends and family. A big bag of thanks to Jupiter Alley and Krystal for their help in making this happen, as well as the team at Wishing Well. Sometimes, the perfect recipe just falls in your lap.